Christmas for the Deputy

Christmas for the Deputy

A Bad Boys of Last Stand Romance

Nicole Helm

TULE
PUBLISHING

Christmas for the Deputy
Copyright © 2019 Nicole Helm
Tule Publishing First Printing, August 2019

The Tule Publishing, Inc.

ALL RIGHTS RESERVED

First Publication by Tule Publishing 2019

Cover design by Michele Catalano

No part of this book may be used or reproduced in any manner whatsoever without written permission except in the case of brief quotations embodied in critical articles and reviews.

This is a work of fiction. Names, characters, places, and incidents are products of the author's imagination or are used fictitiously. Any resemblance to actual events, locales, organizations, or persons, living or dead, is entirely coincidental.

ISBN: 978-1-951190-22-4

Chapter One

IT WAS ENTIRELY possible Penelope Wakefield's greatest secret was that she absolutely *despised* the holiday season. She hated the lights and the songs and the shopping. She hated that, along with all the extra work she was expected to do in the kitchen, she was supposed to let her daughters *help*—which only ever made things twice as difficult, messy, and time-consuming. Everything was a chaotic mess, and Pen *hated* chaos.

But as she woke up the day after Thanksgiving—far too late since she'd been up half the night feeling old and sad and nostalgic and happy and hopeful and *old* after the announcement of her little sister's engagement—she was ready to grin and bear said secret.

She would spend the next six weeks singing Christmas carols, decorating the tree and cookies with her girls, with a big smile on her face. Because she wanted desperately for her girls to grow up loving Christmas and thinking it was magic.

Even if that magic had died for Pen the first Christmas without her mother. But just like then, Pen pretended. So no one would ever know her good cheer was a lie.

That was just the way Pen liked it.

Besides, she had to have *some* hope that her first Christmas living at home in almost twelve years would bring some magic for her girls.

And yourself?

It seemed a bit too much to ask for.

Somehow, despite losing her mother so early, and then losing her husband three years ago when he'd been shot in the line of duty, she managed to look on the bright side of things most of the time. It helped her cope and it helped her feel in control.

But creepy Santa faces seriously, *seriously* tested that control. No doubt his chubby cheeks and lascivious grin would soon be making the rounds.

Pen allowed herself exactly sixty seconds to groan, wallow, and bemoan her lot in life, before she got out of bed. Despite the late hour, she followed her usual morning routine. Make bed, get dressed, check on the girls' rooms to see if they were awake and if they'd made their beds.

She found none of her three girls, and three very, *very* unmade beds.

Frowning, Pen headed for the kitchen, determined to have her first cup of coffee before she started scolding.

But the minute she walked into the kitchen, she noticed the coffeepot was empty and breakfast dishes had been left dirty and scattered about.

Today was so not her day.

She moved to start making another pot when the back door swung open and Ethan marched inside, little Daisy in his arms.

Pen dropped everything she'd been holding and rushed toward her youngest daughter. "What is it?"

"I'm bleeding!" Daisy wailed.

Pen met Ethan's gaze, which was humorous rather than concerned. Thank God.

He settled her onto a chair. "We had a bit of a fall and Daisy scraped her knee. I told her I'd get her all bandaged up."

"Oh, I'll handle it."

"I want Ethan to do it," Daisy said between sniffling cries, clinging to Ethan with a death grip.

Pen frowned at her youngest, who was still crying but looking up at Ethan adoringly through her tears. Daisy was usually wary of strangers, though Ethan was hardly a stranger. Pen's mother had taken him in when Pen herself had been twelve. But Pen had moved to San Antonio with her husband at the age of eighteen, which meant her daughters only knew the three boys Mom and Dad had mentored from visits home to Last Stand. The visits had always been frequent, though, and Ethan was Uncle Ethan to her daughters.

Pen considered Colt, Ethan, *and* Bracken her daughters' uncles, and she knew they did too, but Pen was surprised by how easily Daisy had taken to Ethan in the six months since they'd moved to Last Stand.

"I'll do it," Ethan said, giving Daisy's head a little pat. "Better let the first responder expert handle it." He gave Pen a wink and then went about making a very big deal out of Daisy's very small scratch.

"Now, look how brave you are," he said when the princess bandage was attached to her knee.

Daisy sniffled delicately. "Aren't you going to kiss it?"

Pen watched as Ethan tried to bite back a smile so he looked grave and like he was taking the delicate task of pressing a gentle kiss to her knee very seriously. "There now. Good as new."

"Can I go back and listen to Grandpa's story?" Daisy asked, sliding off the chair. Any trace of tears was gone.

"Yes, but once I've had my coffee all three of you girls are going to make your beds."

Daisy groaned, but she exited the kitchen and out the back door to where Fritz Martin was regaling his granddaughters with tales of who knew what. Pen watched him out the window as he gestured broadly. Her girls—even Addie, the sulky oldest—were giggling and taking great delight in whatever he was saying.

It was good to be home. Pen might not have ever wanted to be involved with the goat farm side of things, but she liked that her girls had chores to do, animals to love. It was good to give her girls their gregarious grandfather on a regular basis. If she reminded herself of that she might come to believe Addie would eventually forgive her for moving them here.

On a sigh, she turned from the window and smiled at Ethan. He was dressed in jeans and a long-sleeved T-shirt, his hair cropped short. When they'd been teenagers, she and her friends had sighed over how *cute* Ethan was. It wasn't the right word anymore. His face was too chiseled, his demeanor too serious. He reminded her of a cowboy in an old black-and-white movie. He just *looked* noble and serious.

"I don't know how you're still single." She went about preparing the coffee machine. "Good job, good-looking, good with kids. If you wait too long to get on that, Daisy will be old enough to make a pass at you before you know it." She grinned over her shoulder at him.

"Maybe that's what I'm waiting for. The chance to be an old pervert."

She swatted his arm and waited impatiently for her coffee to brew. She glanced out the window over the sink to where her father was still telling stories. Meanwhile Colt and Sadie were walking back toward their side of the property.

Pen sighed. She missed the days of having someone to hold hands with. She liked to think she'd come to grips with Henry's death, with the fact she'd always miss him. And she supposed she had because truth be told she was ready for *that* again, even if it wasn't with the man she'd married—thinking they'd be together forever.

The death in 'till death do you part' had come too soon for Henry, and Pen could do nothing but accept that she'd had a good man for too short a time. He'd given her three wonderful daughters.

Besides, her father had lost her mother—the love of *his* life—far too early and he'd been... Well, the first few years had been rough for him, just like hers had been rough for her. But he was happy now, especially now that he was mostly healed from his bypass surgery last summer.

And now her prickly little sister was getting married. *Married.* To Colt Vance, one of Mom and Dad's strays. One of the *Bad Boys of Last Stand.* Which didn't suit Colt now, and had never suited the man in the kitchen with her.

"Aren't they sweet?" Pen murmured.

"Suppose," Ethan replied.

"I gave Sadie a hard time when she first told me." Pen thought uncomfortably to the lecture she'd given her sister about not complicating a delicate relationship. Pen had been wrong, and it ate at her a bit how much so. "I didn't think she knew what she was doing, but I guess she did."

"I guess she did. You don't sound…happy."

Pen shook her head. "I am happy for them. Totally. But, you know, it makes me a little…sad for me. I guess it makes me disloyal, but I can't picture myself like Dad. I don't really want to raise my girls alone. Oh, alone isn't the right word. I have so much help now that we're home, but I… Well, I'm not opposed to getting married again. I miss that kind of partnership."

"Why exactly are you saying it to me?"

She waved it away, and smiled over at steady, stoic Ethan. "You're easy to talk to. You know that. I bet you know half the town's secrets."

He only shrugged, but she knew she was right. She also knew, no matter how much anyone else thought Ethan

Thompson was a simple, good man, he had secrets of his own.

"I don't suppose you know anyone around my age, good with kids, good-looking." She was teasing him, because he so often missed any and all teasing and that always made her laugh.

"I don't suppose I do."

She shook her head and rolled her eyes. Always so clueless was their Ethan. And maybe it was the lack of coffee, or the lack of sleep, but she decided to push it a step further. "You know, I used to have a crush on you."

"I know."

She fisted her hands on her hips in shock and mock outrage. Mostly mock anyway. "Well, now, you've ruined my whole belief that I was subtle about it."

He didn't so much as smile. "Susannah told me."

The mention of her mother deflated Pen's good humor. "She told you I had a crush on you?"

"Yes."

Something about the way he was so *serious* about it gave her an odd sense of foreboding. "I thought Dad was the one who warned you three boys off of us girls." She turned to the coffee and poured, not wanting to look at his stoic expression anymore.

"She didn't warn me off of you."

"Oh, so I was just that repugnant to you?" She gave him an arch look, but he didn't wither or try to backtrack. He merely shrugged.

"If that's what you want to call it." He stood. "Well, I told Colt I'd help him get ready for the cattle. See you at dinner."

With that, he left her more than a little offended.

IT WAS ENTIRELY possible that Ethan Thompson's greatest secret was that he was, in fact, a natural liar. Most people saw his badge, his clean-cut look, and quiet, easy nature as a sure sign he was an honest, straightforward kind of guy.

But Ethan couldn't remember a time when lying wasn't what got him through the day.

Repugnant.

Now, that was a laugh and a half. But Pen had looked at him like she'd believed such ridiculousness. So, he'd lied. And she'd believed him.

He could still remember when Susannah had told him Pen had a crush on him. He'd immediately frozen, so sure Susannah could see some of his less pure thoughts on the matter, and so sure—even then—that the blows would come.

It was his greatest regret in life he hadn't been able to give Susannah the one thing she'd wanted from him before she'd died.

His complete trust.

But in some ways, Ethan wasn't sure he would have learned to trust anyone without losing Susannah first. Now he trusted the entire Martin clan, right alongside his brothers-of-the-heart, Colt and Bracken. Susannah had given them each a gift—in life and in death.

The only person he didn't trust these days was himself.

Because too many things were changing. Sadie and Colt were getting married. Fritz's health, while improving, seemed…perilous. For once in his life Ethan had to look at the man he admired above all else and see him as vulnerable.

But bigger than all those changes, Pen was home. And her girls called him Uncle Ethan and crawled up in his lap, and the ghost of Henry Wakefield didn't hang so heavy. Because Pen had talked about moving on and old crushes.

Ethan blew out a breath in the cold air as he hiked across what would become pastureland for Colt's cattle in the spring. Ethan had been helping out with the cattle prep as much as his schedule at the sheriff's department allowed, and he'd enjoyed himself.

Even if it did mean meals at the Martin house, and Pen bustling around the kitchen looking pretty as a picture. And Daisy wanting *him* to kiss her hurts.

Ethan shook away the simple pleasure he'd gotten out of cleaning up a skinned knee, because it was what he would have done for any kid. Too often adults brushed kids' hurts away as nothing—and he'd vowed never to be the kind of man his father was.

So, Pen might be home, and she might be ready for all life had to offer, but he was still Ethan Thompson. Son of an abusive con man who'd fooled all of Last Stand into thinking he was an upstanding preacher. Until Susannah Martin had done everything in her power to get him out of there.

She has a crush on you, you know.

Ethan practically paused his walking right there as the memory washed over him. Clear and sweet, and with such a potent pang of missing Susannah—the only true mother figure he'd ever known—he wanted to sink to the ground and weep.

Pen is a beautiful, sweet-natured girl with just enough sense of adventure to make her interesting. She'd take care of anyone she loved, fiercely and without reservation. And she'd make any boy a fine partner.

Ethan remembered fidgeting, trying to think of an excuse to run away. It had seemed like such adult talk, and as much as he'd fancied himself an adult, he'd been a skinny and scared fourteen-year-old trying to prove he was brave and tough and that his father's manipulations and abuses hadn't touched him. That the year living under Susannah's roof had made him a different person.

But no matter how many excuses Ethan had made to avoid that conversation, Susannah hadn't let it go.

But you are not that boy. Not yet. Not until you deal with those demons you think you can bury deep inside you.

Ethan had vowed a long, long time ago to never, ever face those demons, but even if he hadn't, Pen Wakefield and her girls were firmly off limits. He would protect them from all that he was. Always.

So, he'd have her believe he thought her repugnant.

He was an excellent liar after all.

Chapter Two

PEN MADE DINNER with a slightly excessive slamming of pots and pans and chopping with perhaps just a little too much vigor. But she had to get her irritation out *some* way, and the great thing about cooking was it either calmed her with its order or it let her bang out all her frustrations without people asking her what was wrong.

"What's wrong?"

Pen nearly jumped a foot and turned to face her baby sister. Mack was standing in the entrance to the kitchen looking vaguely amused, but also...impatient. There was a bag at her feet, because she was planning on leaving and not coming back until Christmas.

Pen sighed. She wished Mack would find what she was clearly searching for out there in the big world, but all Mack ever said was she wanted to be a rodeo star.

Except the rodeo didn't last year-round, and Mack tried to be gone just that.

Pen smiled at her baby sister, the six years between them always feeling like an entire lifetime. "Nothing is wrong."

"You only bang around like that when you're pissed."

"Well, I'm not pissed."

"Liar."

Pen wrinkled her nose, just barely resisting a very mature *am not*. "Aren't you staying for dinner? Where's Bracken?"

"He's not driving me back. I'm taking the train, so I've got to get going, and before you start poking at me to stay home or wait for him or whatever, just…don't."

"Well, fine then," Pen replied. She almost reminded Mack that she'd practically *raised* her those four years after Mom had died and before Pen had moved to San Antonio with Henry, but that just always made Pen a little guilty she hadn't finished the job.

"I do have time for you to tell me why you're having one of your kitchen fits."

Pen gave Mack a killing look as she turned her attention back to her cooking efforts. Then the words fell out of her mouth anyway. "Ethan thinks I'm repugnant."

Mack snorted. "Yeah, and I'm a pretty, pretty princess."

Pen frowned. "What's that supposed to mean?"

"Ethan thinks you're some kind of untouchable goddess. Or Mom's ghost. Or something. But not repugnant."

"He said he did."

Mack shrugged. "He's a liar," she said as if that was a totally *possible* statement.

"Ethan doesn't lie." He took things too seriously, weighed things too heavily, and was far too dedicated to his job enforcing the law to lie.

"Guess he started to," Mack returned. "I gotta go."

"Stay longer at Christmas. And give me a hug."

Mack sighed, but she let Pen engulf her in a hug, and didn't squirm away before Pen dropped a kiss to the top of her head. Just like Mom had always done. Before Mack could slide out the door, Pen took her by the chin. "You look just like her."

Where Pen would have taken that as a compliment, even if it would have made her sad, it seemed to offend Mack unto her soul. "Later, Pen."

"Be safe, Mack."

Mack slung her bag on her back then marched out of the back door. On a sad sigh, Pen turned back to dinner prep.

And couldn't help but think about Ethan *lying*. Surely, that wasn't true. She had never once thought he'd lied to her, but something about Mack's words stuck, haunting her almost. Looking back over old interactions and wondering.

The girls and Dad came in, their usual whirlwind as she scolded them all for lack of cool-weather outerwear and the need to wash up.

Then Sadie and Colt breezed in, Sadie disappearing upstairs to get something, and Colt washing his hands at the kitchen sink, even though she was always on all of them to use the bathroom.

She nudged him out of the way so she could wash her own hands, but since they were alone, she didn't scold him.

"Has Ethan ever lied to you?"

Something strange passed through Colt's expression, but Pen couldn't identify it. "That's kind of an odd question, Pen."

"And that's not an answer, Colt."

He smiled that careless smile of his she didn't fall for so much these days. "Well, now. I guess I don't know about any lying."

Pen thought about arguing with Colt, demanding he tell her the truth, but Ethan was his brother. As much as the boys Mom and Dad had taken in were like family, she didn't have the same relationship with the boys as they did with each other. Despite not having the same parents, they'd bonded like brothers.

Pen had always thought it was sweet, but now it was irritating, because no matter how much she poked at Colt he wasn't going to be honest with her.

The girls raced back in, arguing and laughing in equal measure, as they got to their chore of setting the table. Pen loaded up the table with serving dishes and Dad and Colt took their normal seats. Sadie returned and helped finish with the table.

"Where's Ethan?"

"He's covering someone's shift," Sadie said.

"He could've let me know he wouldn't make it for dinner."

Sadie shrugged. "He told me."

Pen had a million snippy retorts, but she kept them to herself. She looked around the table, almost all of her family situated around it ready to enjoy the meal she'd put together. She should be happy. She should feel fulfilled.

But Mom would have made sure the carrots weren't

quite so roasted. She would have been able to tease Addie out of her perpetual anger about life. She would have braided Daisy's hair so well it wouldn't be a mess of tangles at the end of every day.

Ethan would have told Mom he took someone's shift. Mack would be at this table instead of forever running away.

You will never be Susannah.

She'd been able to live with that in San Antonio. Her mother's ghost had always sat on her shoulders, but here it seemed to stand there with a sledgehammer reminding her of every tiny infraction.

"Pen?" Sadie looked at her with concern, but everyone else was too busy eating and chatting.

"I need some air," Pen managed. She wouldn't cry in front of anyone. Certainly not for something so stupid.

Sadie got up, presumably to come with her, but Pen shook her head. "Please don't."

Though worry dug into lines across Sadie's forehead she sat back down. "Be careful. The porch is icy."

Pen nodded sharply, then quietly got up from her chair. Since she didn't want any company, she went to the rarely used front door. She just needed…a minute. A minute to breathe. To look out at something that wasn't her failure compared to her mother.

She stepped out onto the porch. The night was cold for Texas, and Sadie was right, the porch was icy. The stars twinkled above and Pen hugged herself against…everything.

She took a step forward, being careful—or so she

thought—but her foot only slipped out from under her, sending her pitching backward. She put her arm out trying to break the fall.

The sound of a sickening crack and the sharp blast of pain didn't even surprise her.

It all seemed about right.

ETHAN DIDN'T MIND hospitals, and he was normally pretty calm in a crisis. But as he sat in the waiting room, his stomach churned with nerves.

Fritz entered the room, scowling. He'd been the one to bring Pen in, Sadie and Colt staying back at the farm with the girls. When Sadie had called him about Pen, Ethan had begged the last few hours of his shift off on another deputy.

"Broke her arm," Fritz offered by way of greeting.

Ethan let out a breath. It wasn't so bad. Pen would see it as catastrophic to be so laid up, but broken arms healed.

"Told me to go home. Told me she'd handle it. Stubborn girl."

"Wonder where she got that," Ethan returned.

Fritz only scowled deeper. But Ethan could see the worry, and as much as Fritz had recovered from his bypass surgery, stress was something he needed to be careful about.

"You go home," Ethan said, knowing he was in for a fight but keeping his tone calm and reasonable even if he didn't feel it. "I'll handle it. She'll let me handle it. She's worried about your health, but she'll let me handle things."

"I'm fine and healed and—"

"I know, Fritz. But she broke her arm. She's upset. Let me handle it. She'll feel better about it."

"They're getting a cast on. She didn't want me there." It was the hurt in Fritz's voice that had Ethan laying a hand on his shoulder.

"She doesn't want you to worry, or feel hurt that she's hurt."

"I'm her father."

"And she's our mother hen. She wants to protect you. I know that doesn't set well with you, but let's give her what she wants for right now." Ethan knew Fritz would argue unless he pulled out the big guns. "The girls need their grandpa. They won't believe she's all right from anyone else."

Fritz continued scowling, but he nodded. "She should be released later tonight. You'll bring her home?"

"Of course."

Fritz looked back from where he'd come. "It isn't right."

"It isn't wrong either."

Fritz grunted, patted Ethan on the back, and then headed for the exit. Ethan smiled at the nurse who buzzed him back to the rooms in the emergency wing. When Ethan entered the room, Pen was alone and staring at the ceiling.

"Took quite a spill, huh?"

She looked up at him, then down at the cast like it was an alien life form. Something in her expression was... Well, nothing he associated with Pen. She looked lost, and when her gaze met his, his heart lurched.

"What am I going to do?" she asked, and if it had been anyone else he might have had a good answer. He might not have been so shaken. But Pen didn't ask for help. She didn't ask what to do. She always knew.

Ethan swallowed. She was on painkillers, that was all. He'd reassure her and things would go back to normal. "You'll have plenty of help."

Her eyes filled with tears, but they didn't fall over. "From a man with a heart problem, two people who *just* got engaged, and three daughters under the age of twelve." She nodded as if that seemed about right. "Fantastic."

He moved into the room to stand next to her bed and took her good hand. He gave it a squeeze because the tears she refused to shed just about killed him. "We'll all pitch in. All of us." He didn't mention it was *just* a broken arm. She wouldn't appreciate that.

"Any other day I'd agree with you, Ethan." She sighed, and held on to his hand. "I know I'm being melodramatic, but the month before Christmas? I have shopping and cookies and—"

He couldn't stand to watch the emotional distress cross her face, clear as day. She didn't even try to hide it. "We'll all pitch in. I can handle whatever you don't want to ask your dad or Sadie for. Promise. Whenever you need me."

"It's just…" She looked up at him plaintively. "Daisy still believes in Santa, and Brynn does too—though she tries to act like she doesn't because she wants to be more mature than all that, but she has such an imagination. She can't help but believe. I don't want to drop the ball and ruin that. Not yet."

Ethan's heart twisted. "I promise. Everything will be fine." He'd do whatever it took to make it all okay for Pen. For the girls. "You rest. When they let you out of here, I'll take you home. We're just going to take things one step at a time."

She nodded, swallowing and blinking back those awful tears. "Thank you. I don't know how you got Dad to leave, but thank you. He needs to be home. He needs—"

"For right now, we're just going to worry about what you need, okay?"

She started to argue, but he released her hand and gently pressed her back into the bed. Which was an uncomfortable position, looming over her all laid out on a bed, the blonde strands of her ponytail spread out on the pillowcase.

A hospital pillowcase. A hospital bed, sicko.

"Will you do me one favor?" she asked.

"Anything."

"Wherever that Christmas music is coming from—can you tell them to shut the damn thing off?"

Ethan tried to suppress a smile. "I'll see what I can do." He leaned forward, with half a thought to kiss her forehead. He would have, if it was Sadie or Mack. But...

He straightened instead and headed out of the room to try and find the source of the Christmas music.

It was quite a few hours before they released her. She dozed on the drive back to the Martin farm, but she talked in her sleep.

Lists mostly, of things she had to do. Worries about the girls. She was stressing him out and she wasn't even awake. If that was what was in her head all the time...

Well, she needed help, and she didn't want to take it from her father or from Sadie. He shifted uncomfortably as he pulled his truck in front of the Martin house. Maybe he hadn't planned on being quite so hands on, but he'd dedicated his adult life to helping people. Strangers. Why wouldn't he help someone he cared about?

Pen jerked awake when he turned off the engine, then hissed out a pained breath.

"Easy."

She looked at the house, tears filling her eyes again. She was exhausted, that was all. She'd be fine once she got some real sleep. "They're going to fuss over me."

"What's so wrong with that?"

"I remember when I was eight Mom had pneumonia, and she still did everything for us."

"You don't have to be Susannah."

She immediately moved to open the door, but since her right hand was in a cast and a sling, she struggled to reach across. But she was out of the truck before he could get around to open the door for her.

She trudged toward the house, frustratingly determined.

"Let us help you," Ethan said, coming up next to her.

She moved away from him when he tried to take her good arm.

"I just want to go to sleep."

He'd never heard Pen sound so… He didn't even know the word for it. He'd seen her deal with the death of her mother when she'd been a teenager. The death of her husband, even more cruel and untimely. And yet he'd never seen her so…defeated.

It ate at him, even as he opened the back door and ushered her into the mudroom. She toed off her shoes, using the wall and her good arm for balance. Before they moved into the kitchen, she took a deep breath and something…clicked.

This was the Pen he knew. In control. In charge. Ready to face any challenge.

But he'd seen those moments where she wasn't that at all and had to wonder… Was it all an act?

Pen strode into the kitchen and Ethan followed. Sadie and Colt were sitting at the kitchen table with mugs of coffee.

"I hope you didn't wait up," Pen said.

"No. It's about milking time," Sadie returned, getting to her feet. "Come on. I'll—"

"Please don't. I'm just going to go upstairs and sleep. I don't want to be bothered."

Sadie blinked, opened her mouth to argue as Pen moved through the kitchen toward the stairs. Ethan shook his head and Sadie closed her mouth without a word.

Once Pen was gone, Sadie looked at him. "She's not

handling it so well?"

"Uh. No."

Sadie wrung her hands together. "This is terrible timing. Everything with Christmas and getting ready for the cattle." She looked at Colt, regret in her expression. "Maybe we should move back into the big house until—"

Ethan answered before Colt could agree. "No."

Sadie and Colt looked at him with twin expressions of surprise.

"It'd eat Pen up if you two moved back in here. She doesn't want things to change. She's worried about all the help everyone is going to give her."

"She *needs* help," Colt pointed out.

"Yeah, but we need to be sneaky about it. Listen…" Ethan hated the idea that had popped into his head on the drive home, but the way Pen was acting…

"I'll move into the big house for a bit. My lease is up at the end of the year. I'll tell everyone I'm going to look for a house, but I need somewhere to stay in the meantime so I don't have to sign another year away. That way it's not about her, but I can be here to help out. She'll take help easier from me."

"I'm her sister," Sadie bristled.

"And she doesn't want to be a burden when you and Colt are planning so much. She doesn't want your father stressing himself out worrying over her. But I don't have anything going on. She won't be taking anything from me— she won't see it that way. This will be for the best."

"I guess so," Sadie replied, frowning.

Ethan ignored Colt's considering look and forced himself to smile. "It's settled then. I'll move in and help out, and everything else will go on as it always does."

Colt's mouth quirked. "Sure it will."

Ethan didn't have a clue why that sounded sarcastic, but he didn't want to know.

Chapter Three

PEN WASN'T A baby, and she wasn't a complainer. She was no martyr either. But she wanted to be all three when it came to the cast on her arm.

She'd convinced herself if she'd only broken her left arm things would be fine. But how was she supposed to do it all with a smile on her face when her good arm was in a cast and sling?

She was about to give in to another crying jag before she faced the day—well, what was left of it, but her bedroom door squeaked open and a little head appeared.

Six-year-old Daisy tiptoed in and hopped up onto Pen's bed. Daisy touched Pen's face as if to assure herself Pen was real. Pen felt like a failure all over again. She should have known her girls would be upset. Would need reassurance. After Henry, and even Dad earlier this year, she should have—

"Can I draw on your cast?"

A laugh bubbled up, and God it felt good to let it escape. "Only if you're going to draw a unicorn."

Daisy grinned. "Okay."

"I'm okay, you know that, right?"

Daisy nodded and Pen gave the top of her head a kiss.

Before she could say anything else to reassure her youngest, Brynn bounded in. Her entrance was the complete opposite of Daisy's. She threw the door open so it banged against the wall, and then ran and jumped onto the bed.

Pen grimaced as the jump onto the bed jarred her arm.

"I want to draw on it too!" Brynn announced.

"You'll all get to draw on it." Pen glanced at the door where Addie stood looking anxious.

Pen worried about all her girls, but Addie's behavior gave her the most to worry about. Because Pen recognized hurt and grief and blame. She'd been that girl once, and she didn't know how to fix her daughter.

Not when she still felt all of those things about losing her own mother.

She forced herself to smile at Addie. "All of you," she repeated pointedly.

Pen looked down at Brynn who was bouncing at the end of her bed. "Who braided your hair? It's a mess."

"Ethan did. I think it looks beautiful," Brynn replied with a pout.

"He tried real hard," Addie said, jumping in to defend Ethan.

It was sweet, and she didn't always consider her daughters very…sweet. They'd had a rough few years, and they'd been indulged. Rightfully so, but Pen had started to get worried that they were so caught up in their own loss they didn't think about anyone else's feelings.

Apparently they cared about Ethan's.

"I'm sure he did. But let's fix…" She trailed off because she wouldn't be able to fix any of it with one hand. She was so not used to being out of commission like this, but she would have to find a way to deal with it. "What did you have for breakfast?"

"Aunt Sadie burned the eggs," Brynn said with a giggle. "And said *all* the bad words."

"So Ethan brought donuts," Addie said, giving Brynn a censoring look. "Aunt Sadie didn't mean to. She was trying to help me with my project and she forgot about them."

"I can help you with your project. We still have the weekend."

"Just tomorrow. It's almost bedtime."

Dang it. She'd slept the day away. "Well, tomorrow then."

Addie shrugged and Pen tried not to sigh at her daughter's bad attitude. "I think I've laid around in bed enough. We'll go downstairs and—"

"You're supposed to rest. Sadie said so," Brynn interrupted.

"I have a broken arm—not a broken leg. There's plenty I can still do. And will." Pen nudged Daisy from her side and got out of the bed. Her body ached a bit—her arm a lot. She hadn't slept well, had kept accidentally rolling over on the uncomfortable cast.

But the thought of staying in bed… She shuddered. It would drive her insane. She had to be doing *something*.

The girls trailed after her as she strode out of her bedroom, but she stopped abruptly at the sight of Ethan walking down the hall.

"Oh. I..." She wasn't used to Ethan being upstairs. The boys usually stayed on the first floor when they were at the house, unless one of them spent the night. Which was almost never Ethan. His apartment wasn't so far away. He almost always went home.

Besides, no matter who spent the night, she always had warning. Always made up their beds and knew what to expect. She always...

Always wore a bra. Trying not to draw any attention to the move, Pen crossed her arm over her chest—the arm with the cast not quite cooperating, so she winced.

"Are you going to have the room next to ours?" Brynn asked, hopping in between Pen and Ethan.

"No, stupid. He gets the guest room," Addie returned snottily.

"Don't—" But the admonition to not call each other names was lost as Brynn and Addie faced each other like sparkly little brawlers.

"He's not a guest," Brynn replied, scowling at her big sister. "He's living here now."

"That doesn't mean—"

"Wait," Pen said, with her no-nonsense mom tone that had both of her girls actually quieting. She looked at Ethan, trying to understand what on earth was going on. "You're doing *what?*"

"Temporarily. I'm just staying here temporarily."

"Girls, go downstairs," Pen ordered.

Addie and Daisy immediately headed for the stairs, but Brynn was arguing, asking questions, until Addie rolled her eyes and backtracked and took Brynn's arm. "Come on."

Pen heard her whisper *stupid* again, but Pen could only handle one problem at a time. She waited until she heard the girls clatter down the stairs.

"Before you say anything," Ethan began calmly. "My lease expired."

She gave him the same look she gave her girls when they tried to lie to her. "All of a sudden?"

He offered a sheepish expression. "No. But before you get bent out of shape and think this is all about you, I was going to do it anyway."

"I don't believe you. I never thought you'd lie to me, Ethan." It hurt a little more than it maybe should. But she counted on Ethan to tell the truth. To be…good.

"It's not a lie. My lease is up at the end of the year. I'm too old to keep living in that tiny apartment. Yeah, I'm moving out of the apartment a little earlier than I need to, but only because Sadie was talking about moving back in."

"She can't do that. She has a brand-new life to—"

"Exactly."

She opened her mouth to keep arguing, but he'd boxed her into a corner there. Still, she didn't need him underfoot. She didn't need help. Mom had done it all on her own. This farm. Six kids, more or less, by the time she'd taken in Colt,

Ethan and Bracken. All the while having a career. Pen didn't even have one of those.

Mom had handled all of it without ever breaking a sweat and Pen was determined to be at least half as good as her mother. Which meant she didn't need Ethan's help.

"A broken arm isn't the end of the world. I know I was upset last night, but I'm sure we'll manage."

"You will. And if you need any help, I'll be right here."

"I don't need—"

"Who's going to drag all the Christmas decorations up from downstairs? Who's going to hang the lights outside? Sadie's going to take over cooking—"

Panic squeezed at her lungs. "I don't—"

"If Sadie has kitchen duty, Colt's on goat duty. Your father can help with the shopping and wrapping, but there are some things you need me for."

Need. That was a word she'd learned to hate at a very young age.

But this was Ethan. Needing him was temporary and he was just…Ethan. A steady presence. He'd always be there and he'd always be helpful.

It wasn't *need* so much. More like…pitching in. He was pitching in and she would maybe need his help for a *few* things. Not everything. Not a lot of things. Just the extras. Just for a few weeks because of Christmas.

Besides, arguing with him was pointless. He might dress it all up in a smile and a quiet personality, but Ethan was stubborn. Better to thank him and do her best not to really need him.

"Thank you. You didn't have to give up your privacy. But thank you."

"I'll muddle through. I still have a job I'll be off doing more often than not. I'm not here to be your nanny. Just to help out with a few things."

But he'd done this so Sadie and Colt wouldn't feel obligated to give up their newfound home together. So she didn't feel guilty about asking for help from Dad. Not for *her*, or needing, but because he was helping out the whole family.

She moved forward and used her good arm to give him a hug, before rising to her tiptoes to brush a kiss across his cheek. "Thank you."

He was oddly…tense, but he smiled easily. "You're welcome."

There was something off about that juxtaposition—stiff body, bland expression. She'd always thought Ethan was a straightforward kind of guy, but the past few days made her wonder.

He nudged her to the side a bit. "Gotta drop this stuff off. Save me some dessert, huh?"

She watched him move past her down the hall. She'd never felt like she didn't understand Ethan, but she very much felt that way now.

CHRISTMAS FOR THE DEPUTY

THE ONE POSITIVE to staying at the Martin farm was there was always work to be done. Especially with Colt getting ready to add a head of cattle to his side of things, on top of the work he and Sadie were doing to expand the Martin side of things into a tourist destination. Which was added to their usual producing goat milk cheese the Martin family had been making for almost a century.

On his days off, Ethan could pour his time into moving his body instead of sitting in that house feeling...domestic. And thank God for workdays. He could spend the next two days in his uniform doing what he did best. Law and order and disconnection.

But he still had to get through the rest of today. Right now he got to pound fence posts into the cold ground. Which was much better than yesterday's afternoon fumble through some princess coloring book with Daisy who looked up at him like he'd showered her with gold.

The way she looked at him made his chest feel crushed under the weight of a hundred rocks. Or maybe stampeded by a hundred head of cattle. Nothing good. Nothing good at all.

"You're not really going to let your lease expire," Colt said once they'd gotten through all the posts.

Ethan didn't want to have this conversation, but he knew how to deal with Colt. Don't get defensive. "Why not?" he returned blandly.

"I mean, it's obvious you're doing this for Pen. You don't have to go so far as to lose your apartment."

"I'm almost thirty-two, Colt. Eventually it gets kind of depressing sleeping on a twin bed and not mowing your own lawn. It shouldn't be too hard to find a little house that suits me. Something permanent. Isn't it you who's been telling me for years leasing is just throwing money down the drain?"

Colt studied him, but Ethan didn't have any clue what he was looking for. "We done for the day or—"

"You could build something here," Colt said, his voice low and serious.

Which made Ethan's heart pitch. "Say what?"

"Here. On the property. You don't have to set up shop right next to the cabin or anything, but I've got land, and I know how to build. You could build a little place somewhere on it."

"I…" He didn't know what to say. He was pretty good at defusing a violent or tense situation, good at lying to people about just about everything. But this was simple. "It's not just *your* land."

Colt grinned. "Yeah, you don't think Fritz has been hounding me about offering this for months now? I wanted the time to be right, and I didn't want you to feel beholden. But if you seriously want a place of your own, it should be here. With us."

"Colt."

But Colt only shrugged, as if it wasn't a big deal. "It's a thought. Give it some." He slapped him on the back. "I think we'll call it quits for the day. I've got milking to do, and Sadie asked me to ask you to keep Pen busy during dinner prep so she doesn't drive Sadie insane with her *suggestions.*"

"Right." Ethan couldn't exactly explain why he felt rattled as they walked back to the barn, but he did. Shaken and on uneven footing.

Build a house here. He didn't know how to say no, but the thought was... Well, it was a little too close to some of the things he'd promised himself a long time ago. Then again, so was buying a house, any house.

He wasn't eighteen anymore. He'd learned a few things, and not every promise to himself still served.

But every quiet time in his life eventually ended with something he wouldn't ever want to bring to Martin land. So, this particular thing wasn't possible. He'd just have to find a way to explain that to Colt.

And Fritz, whose car ambled down the drive toward the house, the three girls waving wildly at Colt and Ethan through the back windows. Since Pen wasn't allowed to drive, Fritz had taken over the school runs...and then usually took the girls out for ice cream or candy no matter how much Pen scolded.

The girls' smiling faces and exuberant waves were a good reminder that some of those old promises were still imperative.

"Don't forget. Save Sadie," Colt offered as he took the turn to the barn and Ethan kept heading for the house.

Pen was standing on the back porch, greeting the girls as they bounded inside. She collected their backpacks with one hand, and though he was still out of earshot he could tell she was scolding Fritz about something.

He didn't realize he was smiling until Pen caught sight of him and waved, smiling back.

She looked exhausted, and there was that *pang*. A wistfulness that things could be different.

But they weren't. He wasn't.

Still, when he reached the porch something in him lightened at the fact she'd waited for him.

"Sadie said you two were off building fences."

"Starting to anyway. Long ways still to go."

Pen nodded. She looked like she wanted to say something else, but then she just smiled brightly. "Well, I need to help Sadie with dinner."

He was supposed to keep her occupied, but he knew nothing would work. Nothing except a problem to solve. "I need your advice," he blurted with a wince.

Pen's eyes went wide and she turned to face him. "You do?"

"Uh. Yeah. Yeah, you, um, you give good advice."

"I give excellent advice. Very few people around here solicit it." She stared at him expectantly, but his mind was going conveniently blank. Which didn't at all make sense for a man who was so good on his feet.

"Colt suggested I build a place here."

Pen laughed and rolled her eyes as if it was all old news. She moved to the porch swing and patted the seat next to her.

Ethan sat. He didn't want to talk about this with her since he already knew his answer, but it would keep her out of the kitchen. Sadie was really going to owe him.

"Oh, finally."

"Finally?"

"Dad's been blustering about parceling off land, birthrights and, most importantly, having everyone home."

"I've always been home."

"Last Stand isn't home and you know it. It's the farm or it's nothing. Can you imagine if I'd moved back and bought a house in town? Dad would have had…" Pen wrinkled her nose. "Well, I'd rather not make heart attack parallels given the circumstances, but you know what I mean."

"Sure, but I don't really know what to do." Now, how had the truth tumbled out? He knew what he *had* to do. There was only one option. But part of him ached for something he couldn't have.

And aren't you familiar with that situation?

"Really?"

"That's surprising?"

"I guess I always thought you were the sort who knew their mind."

"I always thought that about you too, until I heard your lists."

Her cheeks went pink and her mouth parted in surprise. "My…"

"You talk in your sleep. Pretty much the whole way home from the hospital."

She didn't say anything to that. Just stared at him, her mouth still slightly parted. Giving him way too many moments to stare back. At the maze of brown and green in her hazel eyes. The strands of honey-blonde hair that wisped around her face.

She was beautiful. She'd always been beautiful.

Last spring he'd told Colt that Colt's feelings for Sadie would fade away. That she'd find someone else. Colt's response about maiming whoever she found had struck Ethan as funny.

He'd watched Pen fall in love with Henry, be his wife and the mother of his children, and there'd been a certain pain in that. But he'd always known it couldn't be him, so he'd been happy for her too. Even with Henry gone, it didn't change that.

So why did he want to touch her so badly?

"Well, anyway. Lists aside," Pen said primly. "You should do it. You know you should. If you're worried about Dad being even more meddlesome, that's just silly. He always finds a way to meddle."

"I'm not even sure what I'm worried about." There. The lies were back where they should be.

"You're family, Ethan. You should be here. Worries or not." She gave his leg a quick pat and stood. "Now I need to help Sadie or she'll do everything wrong."

She got up and Ethan knew he should stop her, but Sadie was a grown woman. She could handle her own sister.

Ethan had to handle his very unfortunate physical reaction to a *leg pat*.

Chapter Four

LONG AFTER EVERYONE had gone to bed, Pen sat in the big living room of the Martin house with her phone balanced in her lap. She painstakingly typed a list into her notes app of everything she needed to accomplish before Christmas.

She was very proud of herself because she was even delegating tasks. Tomorrow she would ask Colt or Ethan to haul the lights out of the basement. Dad was doing school runs, which meant she could ask him to help with the minor homework tasks as well. Since Sadie was doing breakfast these days, she could also pack the girls' lunches when they didn't want to buy.

Pen was totally and 100 percent okay with help. It wasn't currently eating away at her insides like bitter acid. She wasn't constantly remembering what her mother had said to her when she had told her she was dying.

Take care of everyone, baby.

Pen closed her eyes against the wave of pain, tears tripping over onto her cheeks. "I don't know how right now, Mom. I just don't."

One of the stairs squeaked as if someone was sneaking

downstairs. Pen quickly mopped up her face. She wouldn't want one of the girls to be afraid over her crying, or worse be subjected to her father's lame attempts to comfort her.

Whoever it was went into the kitchen and opened the fridge. Then she heard the sound of a can being opened and remembered Ethan lived here now. Unless one of her daughters was sneaking a Coke, she suspected Ethan was sneaking a beer.

Not sneaking. He was old enough and it was perfectly within his right. It was just he'd left all the lights off and was tiptoeing around.

Amused at the idea she got to her feet and moved stealthily toward the kitchen. She pulled up her flashlight app and jumped into the kitchen.

"Busted," she announced shining the light on him. He merely raised an eyebrow, didn't even flinch at the light. She pouted. "You aren't surprised."

"I heard you coming a mile away."

"Cops," she muttered. "What are you doing up?"

"Turns out after almost fifteen years of sleeping in the same bed, I'm not so good at sleeping in a different one. What about you? Let me guess. Worries keeping you awake."

"No," she returned loftily. She tapped the screen of her phone. "Lists. The greatest weapon in the war against stress." She looked at his beer and thought about what else was a great weapon against stress. "Would you do me a favor?"

"Sure."

"Open a bottle of wine for me. Then sit in the living

room and drink with me so I don't feel like a lush."

He hesitated for a moment, but then shrugged. "Sure," he said.

She could have questioned the hesitation, or waved him away and said never mind because she was *fine and dandy*. But he was already moving to the liquor cabinet and pulling out a bottle of wine.

They worked together in the kitchen in relative silence. Ethan opening the bottle for her, Pen pouring her drink. Ethan grabbed a bag of potato chips out of the pantry and raised an eyebrow in silent question.

She nodded, and then they went to the living room and settled themselves on opposite sides of the couch. In silence.

It made Pen itchy.

"You know the first thing I did the first night I was back home? Drank a glass of wine. I hadn't had alcohol in three years, because I got so paranoid if I even had a drink one of the girls would need me to drive them to the emergency room."

"I can't imagine," Ethan returned sympathetically.

She shook her head, not sure why she'd brought that up when it made her sound unhinged. "Therapy helped with a lot...eventually."

Ethan fidgeted on his side of the couch.

"Therapy makes you uncomfortable?"

"Of course not," he said before taking a long swig of beer.

"Hmm. Well, the girls needed it and then...I figured

why not."

"You've dealt with a lot, Pen. No one would think losing your mother and your husband before you even turned thirty would be easy."

Pen shifted a little, because she'd never told her therapist back in San Antonio about losing her mother. It hadn't seemed relevant. More important to focus on Henry and the girls and how to build a new life without suffocating everyone.

"You're really awake because of a different bed?"

He stared down at the can in his hands, something almost haunted in his expression—which was only half illuminated by the light they'd left on in the kitchen. "I'm not Colt. Never could sleep anywhere at any time."

She thought there was a story there, but knew he was not going to be telling it. "Well, I can't wait to get the tree up. Much as I hate Christmas I do love sitting on the couch after everyone goes to bed and watching the twinkling lights."

"You... *You* hate Christmas?" Ethan asked with some mix of surprise and humor.

Crap. She hadn't meant to say that. Well, at least she'd said it to Ethan and not Sadie or the girls.

"Miss everyone has to wake up early and go to the parade?" he continued incredulously. "The endless cookies and carols. You make everyone go to the tree lighting. No matter how long you lived in San Antonio it felt like the month of December you and the girls camped out here. And *you* hate Christmas?"

"It's... Hate is a strong word. I just... It's so much work. And it's so busy. There's no routine, no schedule. I make us do all those things because it's tradition, and that's what Christmas is all about." And maybe, just maybe, because it gave her a sense of order and control in a season that had seemed to be the opposite since Mom had died.

Ethan chuckled and she narrowed her eyes at him.

"You hate it too," she accused.

He sobered some. "I never said that."

"Then why don't you ever spend Christmas Day with us?"

He didn't shift exactly, but his amusement definitely faded. "I work Christmas."

"That doesn't ever stop you on Thanksgiving. Or Christmas Eve. You stop by on holidays you're working. But I never see you on Christmas Day."

He shrugged. And said absolutely nothing else. She sipped her wine and frowned at him, waiting and waiting.

He explained nothing. Just nursed his beer and watched the darkened window.

"You could at least lie. Apparently you're quite good at that." It came out sounding more caustic and accusatory than she'd meant it.

He didn't jolt exactly, but something in his eyes changed. A flash of something, gone so quickly she didn't know what it was. Only that it gave her an odd, foreboding shiver.

She should have paid attention to it, but apparently the wine was doing its job a little too well. "Don't you want to deny it? Tell me how honest and good you are."

"I've never claimed to be honest or good."

She snorted. "Everyone thinks you're honest and good. Everyone thinks you're a paragon of virtue. Gary Cooper in *High Noon* or whatever. You don't have to claim it. You wear it. You *are* it. Everyone thinks so."

"Not everyone."

She knew he meant his father, but then she wondered a little bit if he also meant himself. Which made her feel unaccountably sad. Sad and wanting to fix things.

"Do you remember the year Mom's angel broke?"

His eyebrows drew together, some of his discomfort fading into confusion. "Yeah, but…"

"I broke it. I threw it on the ground and broke it into a million pieces. I hated the sight of it. I hated Christmas without her. I hated everything and I wanted to break all of it." Why was she telling him or *anyone* this?

Because…because she understood. The way you tried so hard to be what everyone else decided you were, and knowing you would never really be that. Being the one person who didn't think you were as good as everyone else did. "I know everyone thinks I'm perfect. I work pretty hard to make sure they do. But I'm not."

"Maybe some people think you are, Pen. But that doesn't mean you have to be."

She could only stare at him. Didn't have to be perfect? Of course she did. Everyone depended on her. Everyone needed her. She was supposed to take care of everyone and how could she do that if they didn't think she was perfect?

Ethan got to his feet. "I should go to bed."

Panic surged through her, God knew why. She'd blame the wine over fear or panic or some unraveling inside of her. "Please...please don't. I don't think I could stand to be alone right now." *But you're always alone, Penelope. Hasn't life taught you to get used to it?*

PEN LOOKED SO pitifully lonely and sad, Ethan had no choice but to sit back down.

He didn't know how this had turned into some awful heart-to-heart. He didn't have a clue what she needed other than a shoulder to cry on. He'd never occupied that space when it came to Pen. Or any of the Martin girls. He was the helper, not the...soother.

Except Pen didn't accept soothing from anyone. Never asked for help or a shoulder to cry on. He'd thought it was because she didn't need it—she'd been right that he had it in his head Pen was something a little close to perfect.

She'd broken her mother's favorite angel. On purpose. Out of anger.

He'd seen her lash out precisely once, and that had been this summer when Colt had been attempting to leave town after Fritz's heart attack. She'd been mad as hell then and had yelled and sworn at Colt.

Ethan figured it had been a one-off. Maybe it was. Maybe it was just the stress of everything lately. Of everything she'd had to go through since Henry had been killed.

"When?" he asked, surprised to find his voice rough.

"When what?" she asked, her voice tight though she wasn't crying. She was holding on to her wineglass for dear life.

"How old were you when you broke the angel?"

She shifted and downed the rest of her wine. "Twenty-five."

His eyebrows rose against his will. He'd been expecting her to say that first Christmas without Susannah. Or maybe even last year or the first year without Henry. Definitely when she was a teenager or as the result of a bad year. Not... When she'd been married and the mother of two.

"I could blame pregnancy hormones, because I was about seven months with Daisy."

"But you don't." That he could tell from the way she said it. From the way she stared at her glass.

"No. I wanted to break it so I'd stop hearing her voice in my head telling me all the ways I did Christmas wrong."

Ethan couldn't believe what he was hearing. "Susannah would never have told you you did Christmas wrong. There's no way to do it *wrong*."

"No. But she would have been here to do it right. I can't ever make it like she did. I can't..."

She was struggling with something bigger than he understood, but the idea she'd stood there at twenty-five, with two kids and one on the way, and thought she could or should make Christmas exactly like it was when her mother had been alive… It cracked something inside of him even if he didn't understand it. "You don't have to be exactly like Susannah, Pen."

"Yes, I do," she replied resolutely.

He didn't understand this. Had never dreamed there was…*this* inside of Pen. "Why?" He knew what it was like to build your life trying *not* to be like someone. But the idea Pen was trying to somehow be Susannah when she was…not… Ethan didn't know what to do with that. Or how to understand it.

"Because I do." She stood and put the empty glass on the side table. "Thank you for staying with me. I'm fine now. Good night, Ethan."

He didn't return the sentiment, just watched her walk stiffly away.

When he woke up later, it was with a start. Still on the couch with a pair of dark eyes staring down at him.

"What are you doing sleeping down here, boy?" Fritz asked. Fritz frowned at the beer can. And the wineglass next to it.

Ethan cleared his throat. "I didn't mean to," he said, feeling like a scolded teenager.

"I woke you up because you've got to work today," Fritz replied. "And maybe so you could help me with that damn coffee maker I can't make head nor tail of."

Ethan pushed himself off the couch, ignoring the crick in his neck. "Sure." He followed Fritz into the kitchen and then set about making the coffee. It was still dark out, and when Ethan glanced at the clock he was a little surprised to see it read four a.m.

"You're up early," Ethan offered, putting together everything he'd need to brew a big pot of coffee for everyone.

"Thought I'd help with the milking this morning." Fritz settled himself at the table. "Not like you to mix your liquor, boy."

"I didn't..." Ethan trailed off, because of course Fritz knew exactly who'd been drinking out of the wineglass. He didn't know exactly why Fritz was pointing it out though, so he kept his mouth shut and poured the coffee grounds.

"I suppose you remember the promise you made to me after Susannah died?" Fritz said conversationally. But Ethan knew this was no conversation. He wasn't sure what it was going to be, but it was pointed. Purposeful.

"Of course I do."

"You made yourself into a good man, and took absolutely no help or gifts from me, which still offends me, by the way."

Ethan might have smiled if he didn't feel dread seeping through him as he pushed the coffee buttons.

"A man of the law. Trusted and respected. I couldn't have asked more of you. I'm proud of you. Susannah would be extraordinarily proud of you."

"Thank you," Ethan managed, even though he knew it wasn't true. Oh, Susannah would have been proud about his profession. It was half of why he'd decided to become a cop.

But she wouldn't be proud of *him*. There'd been so much more she'd wanted out of him.

So much he didn't want for himself.

"But the other side of that promise, I don't hold you to that anymore, if that's what you're worried about. Colt and Sadie aren't a special case. I trust you, Ethan."

But I don't. "Fritz, it's nothing like that." Colt hadn't wanted to get mixed up with Sadie because Fritz had made all three of his boys promise not to touch his daughters after Susannah had died.

Colt had always figured it was because Fritz didn't want broken men like them loving his precious daughters, but Fritz had explained it was about wanting to keep the family together. Romantic entanglements could lead to breakups and Fritz being put in the difficult decision of choosing between his God-given daughters and the boys he'd basically raised after Susannah had saved them.

Colt and Sadie had worked through those issues, promised forever to each other, and that was all well and good. But it wasn't Ethan's hands-off promise to Fritz that held him back when it came to Pen.

"What's it like then?" Fritz asked.

"I just want to help out."

"The broken arm will hold her back some, but this is Pen. She's stronger than the lot of us times ten. Three years after Susannah died I was just barely crawling out of rock bottom. Not my Pen. She's got those girls home and is happy as a clam. Don't go babying her. She won't like that at all."

Ethan opened his mouth to argue, then decided to shut it. He didn't want to baby Pen, and Fritz was probably right that she wouldn't like being babied.

But Ethan had a bad feeling she needed it.

There was a crash and the clatter of little feet on the stairs. Then Brynn appeared, all but doing a cartwheel into the kitchen. It took Ethan by surprise just one of the girls made *that* much noise all on her own.

One of the three perfectly wonderful and adorable reasons nothing would ever, *ever* happen between him and Pen.

Chapter Five

PEN AVOIDED ETHAN for most of the day. Luckily, he was working today which meant she didn't have to work too hard at it.

She didn't know what had possessed her to tell him the truth. When he'd said she didn't have to be exactly like Susannah she should have said *of course not*.

She was forever telling someone *of course not*, then changing the topic. Telling Sadie how to cook dinner, or her girls to do a chore.

She'd told Ethan about the angel, and that she had to live up to her mother's impossible memory. And now she had to go on with Christmas prep like it didn't matter. Like she wasn't falling apart.

Don't you have ample experience in that department?

Yes, yes, she did. The trick was to always, always go on the attack.

Colt had dragged up the Christmas decorations and Pen had convinced Sadie to leave her goats and cheese for an hour to come help her sort through things before the girls got home.

"Mack should be here," Pen announced. Mack could be

her new project. One a broken arm couldn't stop. She could work on convincing her baby sister to come home—not just for Christmas but for good.

"She'll be here for Christmas."

"Are we ever going to do anything about her?"

Sadie snorted. "Do you *know* our baby sister? Even *you* can't do anything about that particular force of nature."

"I'm quite sure I could," Pen replied with a sniff, not at *all* sure. Mack was…Mack. Pen considered herself an excellent maneuverer, but some people defied maneuvering. Mackenzie Martin was top of that list.

Sadie gave Pen a placating smile, which had Pen frowning. *She* was the one with the placating smiles. Not Sadie.

"She'll come home when she's ready. Just like you did."

The fact Sadie was right only made the low-level panic her old therapist would remind her was anxiety, not reality, cinch its knot tighter.

There had to be something she could fix. Something she could accomplish.

"Does Colt know why Ethan never comes over on Christmas Day?"

Sadie shrugged, as wholly unconcerned with that as she was with Mack gallivanting throughout Texas barely ever coming home. Pen ground her teeth together.

"If he knew, he wouldn't tell me."

"You're going to be his wife."

"Yeah, and Ethan is his brother. Colt only just got to telling me more about his childhood since we've been together. I'm sure Ethan has things he'd rather not face."

Pen frowned. Ethan's home life had been...awful. And even though his father had moved away from Last Stand before his scandal with a young parishioner had gotten him arrested, she imagined Last Stand still had something to say about it.

Pen frowned deeper. It had happened while she'd been in San Antonio. Before that she vaguely remembered some rumor about her mother running Abe Thompson out of town. But nothing more than whispers had ever come of it, and then Susannah had died and she'd become something of a saint to the people of Last Stand.

Ethan was liked and respected as well. She didn't remember any visits where he'd been upset over his father. Besides, he'd cut himself off from his family before all that. Clearly it hadn't really mattered to him.

What would he have to hide?

I've never claimed to be honest or good.

"What's wrong?" Sadie asked.

"Nothing." Sadie didn't need to know Pen had pegged Ethan wrong all these years. "Dad should be back with the girls, don't you think?"

Sadie laughed. "It's Friday. I bet he took them to get ice cream."

Pen wrinkled her nose. "Or to the candy store."

"Or both," Sadie continued.

"How am I ever going to teach them any discipline with Dad spoiling them?" Pen groused.

"If you were really worried about that, you wouldn't have moved home. They're good girls."

"They are." She knew how lucky she was. Henry's death had been hard, really hard, but none of the girls had acted out terribly or behaved in a way that made Pen overly worried about their emotional well-being.

Addie sometimes reminded her a bit too much of herself, but Brynn was as exuberant as ever, and Daisy was a shy little thing. But they were good girls. Who could probably stand a little spoiling from their grandfather.

"I suppose you'll make them get up early to make sure we visit every Christkindlmarkt booth?"

"Naturally."

"Remember the year Mom overslept for the parade and swore a blue streak trying to get us ready?"

Pen stared at her sister. "What? No. You dreamed that."

"I did not," Sadie returned indignantly. "Trust me. You remember the first time you hear your mother drop an f-bomb."

"Mom would *never*."

"Well, it was hardly the only time I heard her swear."

Pen didn't know why she was getting so angry, but Sadie was wrong. Completely and utterly wrong. "You have lost your mind, Sadie Martin. Our mother did not swear. At least not in front of us. Stop making things up."

Sadie frowned at her. "I'm not making it up, Pen. What's your deal?"

"I won't let you talk about her that way. I won't listen to

it." Pen got to her feet.

"Pen. Come on. You're being ridiculous."

Pen stormed out of the room. She was not being ridiculous. Sadie was ridiculous. And a liar. Pen flung open the front door and stomped onto the rarely used porch where she'd fallen and broken her stupid, useless arm.

She was shaking, and it was getting harder and harder to suck in a breath. What was wrong with her? Was she having a heart attack like Dad?

Except her chest didn't hurt. She just couldn't breathe. Why couldn't she breathe?

"Pen?"

God. Ethan was not what she needed right now. It made the not being able to breathe worse. It made everything worse.

He took her by the elbow and sat her down on the rocking chair. Gently he nudged her head between her knees.

"Count to ten, sweetheart. Slow, with each breath. Focus on your shoes. In, one, two, three..."

She managed to suck in a breath as he counted, then one out as he reversed the numbers.

"Ten, nine, eight..."

He made it worse and fixed it, all at the same time. Slowly the panic eased, the pressure disbanded. Still, she kept her head between her knees because *oh God*.

He kneeled in front of her like she was a child. Or someone he was dealing with on a call. He was in his uniform still, so it suited all in all. "What's all this?" he asked gently.

"Nothing." Nothing. She'd lost it, but she'd get it back together. She'd fix it with Sadie and—

"It looks a bit like a panic attack, sweetheart."

"I'm not your sweetheart," she snapped, lifting her head. "And I don't have panic attacks. And my mother didn't swear!" She was seriously losing it. And Ethan was just *there*, being all calm. Which was *her* job.

"I-I. I apologize. I was just..." She couldn't even come up with a good excuse.

"You don't have to apologize," Ethan said, and his voice was warm and soothing but completely devoid of emotion. Cop to hysterical victim. "Adults can have breakdowns too."

"It's not a breakdown," Pen said, doing her best to sound calm and in control. "It's not a panic attack. I was upset. I'm better now. Thank you."

Ethan took her hand in his, and then the other. He gave them a squeeze, just squatting there like it was an easy pose to hold. When he met her gaze, some of that detachment had faded into a warmth that almost made her feel better.

"It's okay to be having a rough time."

She really wanted that to be true, but it was dumb. She hadn't been this out of control after Henry had died. Anxious and devastated. But she'd held it together for her girls. For her babies.

Why would she fall apart *now*? She'd healed as much as someone could in three years. She was home. Things were as good as they could be.

That thought made her want to sob. Why didn't she feel

good? "I don't understand. Everything... Everything is as it should be."

He rubbed his thumbs over her knuckles, a sweet, caring gesture. A man-to-woman gesture that lightened the weight in her stomach and created a little buzz against her skin, especially while she held that brown gaze of his.

"Sometimes it's when everything is as it should be that we have to deal with the things we haven't yet."

"I dealt with losing Henry. I had to. I had therapy, Ethan." She wanted to sound condescending but she was pretty sure she just sounded desperate.

"What did you mean before? When you said that your mother didn't swear?"

"I..." Pen blinked. Everything lately had been about her mother, hadn't it? And a creeping anxiety she remembered from the first few months after Henry's murder had taken over, but this time her anxiety wasn't about the girls' safety or even her own. It wasn't about leaving the house or going to sleep.

It was all about living up to Mom.

She'd dealt with losing her husband. In part because of therapy, in part because of her girls, and in part because she was old hat at grieving. She knew what it was to lose someone and always feel sad and jilted over it.

She'd *accepted* that when it came to losing Henry, especially the way she had, but had she ever accepted it when it came to losing her mother?

She stood up abruptly. "I have to go inside." She managed to tug her hands out of his though it hurt her broken arm. She turned away from him. She needed...space. She needed to be alone. She needed...

A million things she didn't have time for. She rushed inside, only ran smack dab into her father.

"My office, girl."

"Dad. You're home." She forced herself to smile at him. She could fool her father. She'd been doing it for fifteen some years.

"Now," he said in that voice that brooked no argument. The one he pretty much only used on Sadie and Mack. Since he almost never used it on her, she didn't know how to fight it.

So, she walked with him to his office. He pointed to a chair in front of his desk. She took it, working on excuses and assurances.

He took the seat behind his desk, looking big and imposing with the rolling hills out the window behind him. The sun was setting, earlier and earlier every day. A depressing thought.

"Your sister is worried about you."

Pen plastered a smile on her face. "No need for that. I was just getting sentimental. You know how Christmas is."

"That's not what she explained to me."

Maybe Sadie should keep her big mouth shut.

"She said you got upset over the idea of Susannah swearing."

"Daddy..." She didn't know how to explain, and he

looked so sturdy sitting there. Not pale and weak like he'd been after his surgery. It reminded her of before. Before Mom had gotten sick when she'd thought her father had to have hung the moon.

"I've been thinking about Mom lately. A lot." The words sounded foreign to her ears. Telling her father this was unprecedented. She didn't talk to him about missing Mom because it upset him.

Fritz sighed. "Christmas always does that for me. She loved the tree lighting. Loved all of it. I miss her always, but a little more this time of year." He sounded wistful, but not as pained as he had years ago.

"It's not missing her. It's..." Pen swallowed. Why was she even considering laying this at her father's feet? He had his own grief, his own stress, his own—

"I know you've always tried to fill her shoes," Dad said gently.

Tried. Which meant failed.

"She told me I had to. She... The last thing she said to me... Take care of everyone, baby. That's all I'm trying to do. I got a little upset is all. But I'm taking care of everyone even with this stupid thing and—"

"You..." Dad shook his head and got to his feet. He crossed the room and practically lifted her out of her seat and engulfed her in a tight bear hug that had her wincing at the discomfort in her arm.

"What?" she asked into his shoulder, the sound muffled.

He pulled back. His eyes were brimming with tears,

which wasn't unusual when he spoke of Susannah. "That was one of the last things she said to me, too. 'Take care of them, Fritzy. You have to take care of all of them.'"

"Me too."

Pen jolted in Dad's arms and turned to find Sadie standing there, tears in her eyes but none having fallen over.

"What?" Pen demanded. That didn't make sense. Mom had entrusted *her* with the caring.

"'Take care of your father and the farm. Be good to your sisters.' Daddy didn't want me in there that last day, so she was still kind of lucid when I talked to her."

"I don't..."

"She wanted us *all* to take care of each other, darlin'. Not you to shoulder all that weight."

Pen sank back into the chair now that her father wasn't holding her. She didn't understand how...

"I should have seen it. You were so strong, too strong, and I was a mess. So I... I leaned too much on you."

"Don't blame yourself," Pen said immediately. "Not ever. You did the best for us. You always have."

"Not always," Dad said, sharing a look with Sadie.

Which was about stupid farm stuff. Not important stuff. Not family stuff. Oh, Pen loved the farm—she did. But not the way Sadie and Dad did, like it was some kind of limb they couldn't live without.

"I was just upset is all."

"You had a panic attack," Sadie countered.

Pen opened her mouth to argue, then wondered why.

Why was she trying to prove she didn't have some unresolved feelings about losing Mom? About being the caretaker?

Mom had asked *all* of them.

"I think we all did a pretty good job of taking care of one another then," Fritz said. "We won't stop now. You will ask for help, young lady. You will talk to someone when you're sad. Let the rest of us handle Christmas."

"I am. I had Colt bring up the decorations and Sadie was going through them with me. You take the girls to school. I sit around doing *nothing*."

"You should relish a little nothing. Even before Henry died, you did a lot of the heavy lifting with those girls due to his hours. He was a good man, a good father, but a lot fell on you. Take a break. Be a little lazy."

"Lazy? I wouldn't even know how." The thought *terrified* her to her soul.

"You couldn't breathe, Pen," Sadie said softly. "I've never seen anyone get so pale. You've got to take it easy. On yourself. You're the only one who holds yourself to some impossible standard."

"Mom was…" *The impossible standard. I can't be her. I can't even come close.*

"Susannah wasn't perfect," Dad said, and Pen's mouth dropped open. She saw Sadie's had too.

Dad cleared his throat. "She was perfect *to me*. But she did in fact swear. At me, usually. Sometimes she got so wrapped up in a case she'd forget to eat, or tell you three to do your homework. She didn't tell anyone she was sick until a month after the doctor told her. Your mother had her faults. She was wonderful, and everything to me. But trying to be her is silly. You're you. And that's just what we and your girls need."

Pen wanted to believe it. She knew she should.

"I'm tired," was all she managed to say.

"Take a nap," Sadie said with an encouraging smile. "We can handle everything. I promise."

So, for the first time in her life, Pen ignored her responsibilities and let someone else take care of them.

Once she got into bed, she fell asleep immediately.

Chapter Six

ETHAN TURNED THE can of Coke over in his hands. Even though he was sitting out under the stars with Colt, he couldn't get the picture of Pen pale and gasping for breath out of his mind.

"You going to drink that or spray it all over?"

Ethan looked down at the can and grimaced. He set it down on the patio. He hadn't come over to Colt and Sadie's cabin for the fun of it. Not even to try and keep away from Pen, though it wasn't a bad side effect.

He had to be clear and concise and not let this *maybe* hang between them. Not on the house issue. "I can't take you up on your offer, Colt."

Colt kicked his legs out in front of him and crossed them at the ankles. He didn't say anything as he stretched his arms out and then folded them behind his head.

"You can't take my offer to help you build a cheap house on family property?"

"It's not my family's property. You know..." Ethan didn't want to go into this. Didn't want Colt jumping into protective brother mode. But it was important Colt understood this wasn't a slight. It was just reason.

"My father will go after me when he gets out."

"And he'll go right back to jail where he belongs if he does anything."

"Maybe," Ethan agreed. But he also knew the law could be twisted and manipulated by lawyers and judges. His father would have gotten away with forcing himself on that teenager if the girl's parents had had any say in it. They were too embarrassed to press charges. When a friend at the police department handling his father's case had told Ethan what was going on, Ethan had done his level best to work with everyone he could to convince that poor girl to press charges.

She finally had. But his father's sentence was insulting at best. Five years. It should have been ten for the age gap. More for manipulating that girl into thinking she'd been asking for it.

Ethan tried not to be bitter about it. The justice system was unfair. Always had been and always would be. He tried to take pride in the fact he'd had something to do with getting his father put behind bars, even if it wasn't long enough. It was something to be proud of because no one, not even Susannah, had been able to do that.

But Ethan had no doubt his father would find a way for revenge. Only he'd pretty it up in scripture and talk about vengeance and not sparing the rod. In his pulpit, he'd been an engaging minister with a loyal flock.

At home, he'd twisted the words of the Bible to suit his whims, and his punishments. And he knew how to make people think *they* were the ones in the wrong no matter what.

Ethan might be an adult with a badge, but his father was the kind of man who knew how to hurt people. And it wouldn't be Ethan he hurt. It would be the people Ethan loved.

"I don't want to be living this close. The Martins and you already have a big X on all y'all's chest for Susannah helping me get out of there, for Susannah running him out of town. Put me on your land? It's asking for trouble."

"Then I'll ask for it. Because you're my brother and I don't plan on being scared of your daddy. Just like Susannah wasn't."

If it had just been Colt, Ethan would believe him. He'd trust his brother to do all the protecting. But it wouldn't be just Colt soon enough. "What if you and Sadie have kids?"

"Well, we are in fact planning on that…eventually. I don't see what that's got to do with anything."

Ethan wanted to smile at the discomfort in Colt's tone, though he tried to hide it. But there was nothing funny about this. Nothing funny about risking Colt's future.

"He could use them. Use the girls. He's… He isn't like your father was, Colt. He's not a drunk and he's not angry. He's calculated. He got Amy committed. She wasn't crazy. She didn't need to go to that place. She needed to get away from him, but he made her…" Ethan was getting too lost in old things. He needed to focus on the facts. On the now.

"It's a shame about your sister, Ethan. But I'm not a teenage girl."

Ethan took a deep breath and let it out. "But you might *have* teenage girls." He forced himself to meet Colt's frustrated gaze in the dim porch light. "I'm a cop, Colt. I'd like to believe I can save everyone, but I know I can't. Instead, I know what men like my father can do. Will do."

"You can't let him dictate your life."

"If I did I wouldn't be here. I would have gotten out of Last Stand and away from everyone I loved a long time ago. This isn't letting him dictate my life. It's taking necessary precautions. It doesn't guarantee that he won't still try to hurt someone I care about to get at me. I'm not being a martyr here. I'm being as reasonable as I can."

Colt didn't say anything. He didn't have to. There was nothing to say unless he wanted to keep arguing against reality.

"I'm going to head back." Ethan stood to walk back across the land between Colt's cabin and the Martin farmhouse. "I'll extricate Sadie and send her home to you."

But Colt hadn't quite given up on the conversation. "It isn't right, Eth."

Ethan winced a little at the pain of that, but luckily he'd stepped into the dark so Colt wouldn't see it. "No. It isn't fair. Neither is life. We both know that. Not much you can do about it."

Colt muttered something that sounded an awful lot like *we'll see*, but Ethan knew arguing wouldn't change anything. He'd keep the course and always do his best to protect the people he loved from anyone who might wish him or them harm.

The end.

He walked back to the Martin house, taking his time even though it was a cold December night. The stars were bright and though it was winter, life teemed around him. Because life always kept going on, no matter what happened.

When he finally made it to the house, Pen was sitting out on the stair of the back porch. She was alone, the windows behind her shining bright, but she was wrapped up in a blanket because it was darn cold out.

"What are you doing?"

She smiled a little sheepishly. "Well, after this afternoon it might surprise you to know everyone is treating me like I might break. So, I'm watching the stars and trying not to go crazy and clean the whole house one-handed to show them what's what." She patted a spot on the stair next to her.

He didn't want to take it, but he did so anyway.

"I just wanted to thank you for this afternoon."

"Well, that's stupid." He hadn't meant to snap, but thanks always irritated him. Thanks from her made him downright pissed.

She made a huffy sound, which almost amused him enough to take away the pissed. But the last thing he wanted was her thanks.

"It isn't stupid. I know you would have done it to any stranger on the street, believe me, I can tell the difference between *cop* and *Ethan*."

"There's a difference?"

"To me there is. Between Mom and Henry and you, I learned to tell the difference pretty easily. And that's who you were—cop. But I needed someone to be that instead of... Well, someone I have to take care of. I don't have to take care of you."

Something lodged in his chest and he really didn't know if it was a good feeling or bad feeling, just that it was *stuck* there, a weight against his lungs. "No, you don't."

"I guess I have some unresolved...mom things."

"Who doesn't?" Ethan muttered.

"I'd ask about yours, but you won't tell me."

"It doesn't matter." Nothing about the time before Susannah really did.

"Of course it matters. But I understand not wanting to... Well. I understand." She made a pained face. "Sometimes telling yourself it doesn't matter doesn't make it so. And sometimes you deal so well with some things, because you never dealt with others."

"Will it do me any good to repeat what I said the other night? You don't have to be Susannah. No one expects you to be."

She sucked in a breath. "I need to hear it, I guess. I think... I think I turned missing her into wanting to be her."

"There are worse things."

"I just thought coming home was right. I was so sure everything was good. But I don't feel good." She blew out a breath like it was some great, horrible admission. "And I don't want my daughters to know that. I don't want Sadie or

Dad to know that. I know they'd love me anyway, but…I want to be the strong one. The one in control."

Those words echoed inside of him, reminding him of old feelings, old desperate wishes that he thought had died long ago.

"I thought it was my personality, because it was the last thing she said to me. She told me to take care of everyone. So, I latched on. Like doing it could keep her alive even though I knew it couldn't."

The days after losing Susannah had been especially dark. Fritz had been inconsolable, the girls had been so young, and he and Colt and Bracken had been so…worried. Worried they'd have to go back to who and what they'd been before Susannah had saved them.

But that had been a long time ago. In the here and now Pen had to finally understand she didn't have to be the only one taking care. "Last thing she said to Bracken, too."

"What?"

"She asked him to watch out for you girls. You don't think he trails after Mack for fun, do you? Or it's a coincidence they find themselves on the same rodeo circuit."

"I…" Pen blinked and then let out a sad little laugh. "Well." She seemed to think that over, but didn't seem upset about it. Not really. Still, she was serious as she watched the moon rise. "Dad and Sadie too. I suppose she said it to all of us."

He shook his head slowly, wishing he didn't have to picture that *last* all over again.

"She didn't say it to you?" Pen demanded.

"No," Ethan said, hoping that would be it. Even knowing it wouldn't be.

"So what did she say then?"

"She said…" Ethan blew out a breath. "'I'm sorry I have to go so soon.'" But she'd never asked him to care for anyone, look out for anyone. And Ethan had always known why.

Susannah had wanted to save him, *had* saved him. She'd blackmailed his father into leaving town without Ethan, but she hadn't been able to *beat* Abe Thompson. She hadn't been able to arrest him or prove anything he'd done.

Mostly thanks to Ethan's mother refusing to corroborate anything Ethan said, claiming both her children were in desperate need of a mental health evaluation.

Ethan might have been saved thanks to Susannah knowing enough of her father's secrets to make him wary, but not enough to put Abe behind bars. Ethan wasn't free from his father's reach or his father's name.

So she'd only been able to apologize to him, knowing she was dying. She hadn't asked anything of a man so connected to something so bleak.

It took him a while to come out of that memory, to remember where he was and who he was with. To regret he hadn't changed the subject or made something up.

Because Pen was crying.

"I'm sorry. I didn't mean to make you sad. I just—"

She waved him off. "I asked. I needed to know. I… I put it all away to take care of everyone else, and now I guess I have to let it all out." She sniffled miserably, a little sob escaping her mouth after that. "And I don't want to cry in front of anyone else."

He'd known his whole life how cruel words could be, but those might be the cruelest he'd ever heard. All the things he wanted wrapped up in all the things he couldn't have.

But for a second or two, he had to be what she needed. For Pen. "Shh, now," he said, wrapping his arm around her shoulder and pulling her close. "You don't have to." He didn't want her crying in front of anyone else if it meant he got to comfort her.

You shouldn't.

But even that voice inside his head couldn't argue with a crying woman.

She sniffled and nestled in, wrapping her good arm around him. So, he held her while she cried and tried not to let his mind wander. Or worse, dream.

"The nice thing about the police is you can almost always be guaranteed they've seen way worse than your emotional breakdown," she said in a squeaky voice, her cheek pressed to his chest and her arm holding him tightly.

Not tight enough to blame this crushing sensation in his chest on, but it'd go away. It'd go away eventually.

"We have indeed," he responded, baffled by how rusty his voice sounded. Since he *was* a cop, he had held more than one stranger while she cried over a variety of things. He'd seen people rage over awful things. This was a little blip of a nothing when it came to the emotional outbursts he'd seen.

But it was Pen, so it hurt him to see her hurt.

She let out a shaky breath and straightened her shoulders, releasing him slowly. "Emotional release is good for grief," she said, as if reciting a poem. "A natural response to loss."

Ethan didn't know what to do with that—he imagined some words her therapist had given her to deal with Henry's death.

It all settled very uncomfortably, like the sound of nails on a chalkboard making his skin prickle. *Emotional release.*

Controlling it was a far better response. What kind of cop would he be if he responded *emotionally* to things?

But she wasn't a cop, so those words were probably quite helpful for her and that was fine. Just fine. He didn't need to give in to the desperate impulse to move away from her. To talk about something else—*anything* else.

Slowly he withdrew his arm from her shoulders, trying to act casual. Trying to feel casual.

"I'm sorry. That makes you uncomfortable."

"What does?"

"Talking about dealing with emotions. Don't take this the wrong way, but the bad boys of Last Stand aren't exactly known for their soft, emotional sides." She smiled sweetly, as if it would soften the blow.

But it wasn't a blow. That was a compliment as far as he was concerned.

"Colt's better now. Which just goes to show, you and

Bracken need a good woman in your lives."

"I don't…" He didn't know how to finish that. *Need a woman* seemed a little harsh, even if it was true. She'd only set about trying to find him one. He barely repressed a shudder at the thought.

"It's so weird. I thought losing control would be the worst thing, sometimes that thought still creeps up on me, but…I feel lighter than I have in years. I know the worst thing isn't the girls seeing their mother cry or Sadie making a dinner or two. The worst thing is losing people you shouldn't have to, but we all do anyway."

"So, that panic attack was some kind of godsend?" he asked incredulously. It was hard to believe Pen thought breaking down was *good*.

She thought about it. "I suppose." She huffed out a soft laugh. "I don't magically feel *better*. I just don't feel so tightly wound. And I remember that from after Henry died. Some of the exercises the therapist gave me and the girls helped with that panic and anxiety. It's strange to have some of those feelings again and not recognize them. But I know how to fight them now… I think. That makes me feel less…out of control. To apply some of the things I did after we lost Henry to these feelings about Mom."

Ethan opened his mouth to say something, but he realized he didn't need to. She was dealing with some big stuff, and it was the kind of big you had to unwind on your own. She just needed someone to be a shoulder to cry on every now and again.

It didn't bother him any to take on that role.

She patted his leg.

Well, maybe it bothered him a *little*.

"You being here helps too. You've always been the steady one. I never had to worry about you." She smiled up at him.

It was meant to be a compliment, and he knew he should take it as one. He wasn't her burden to bear. Good deal.

But she wasn't...the grand holder of worries in the Martin clan. She wasn't... "You know everyone here worries about you."

She blinked at him, her eyebrows drawing together. Not just as if she was rejecting what he said, but as if she didn't understand it.

"No matter how much they've always thought you had it all together. Your father worried about you leaving home so young. Sadie and Mack worried about you trying to raise three kids on your own after Henry died. Colt and Bracken threatened Henry before he asked you to marry him."

"They *what?*" she screeched.

"Henry never told you?"

"He told me they had a chat." Pen frowned deeply. "He said it was friendly. About his intentions. He said he told them he was going to marry me and they congratulated him."

Ethan couldn't help a smile. "They said they'd hunt him to the ends of the earth if he ever hurt you."

She made an offended sound, then narrowed her eyes at him. "And what did you do?"

Ethan looked down at his hands. He hadn't wanted to get involved. Not with...that. "I didn't approve of threats, so they went when I was at work."

"Why does it feel like there are all these things no one ever told me?"

"Because there are always things people don't tell each other. Everyone has their own...secrets is a harsh word. But you know, separate things."

"I suppose you are full of *separate things*."

"I suppose I am." And he wasn't ever going to share them with *her*.

"I don't want anyone to worry about me," she said resolutely, as if saying it would make it so. "I never wanted that. Not from any of them."

"But the people who love you always will. That's kind of part and parcel of the whole family and loved ones thing."

She looked up at him. She studied him as if she could read his mind, and she was quiet and studying long enough he wanted to fidget.

He made a move to get up, but she took his hand in her good one. She held him there, still studying him. Still quiet.

He forgot about the cold night and the emotional upheaval, because it wasn't often someone focused on *him*. He preferred to keep himself more in the background. He was there. He could be counted on and leaned on.

But not looked at and *into*.

Especially when she leaned closer, when her eyes seemed to decide *something*.

Her mouth moved toward his, and even though every inch of his chest ached to move forward—to lean in and accept—the rest of his body knew what that could cost. And he panicked.

He jumped up and she fell a little forward, just barely catching herself with her good arm. She glared up at him.

He couldn't let her glare or talk or anything. He had to pretend this hadn't happened. He lunged forward, almost tripping over his own stupid feet. He caught himself with the banister. He might have had room to be embarrassed if he wasn't so absolutely sure he had to get away. Now. And pretend that had never happened.

"Ethan—"

"Night, Pen." Maybe it was an embarrassing overreaction of an escape, but it was necessary. Vital.

Because if he'd let her kiss him, it would ruin everything.

Chapter Seven

PEN HAD NOT slept well, but she didn't plan on discussing that with anyone. She got the girls up, though Addie grumbled about getting up and going on a *Saturday*.

"But it's the Christmas parade and then Christkindlmarkt. You love Christkindlmarkt."

"*You* love Christkindlmarkt. It's just dumb crafts."

Pen moved out of her daughter's room, rolling her eyes. No, she actually didn't love the Christkindlmarkt. Because it reminded her of Mom. Of magic Christmases where Pen didn't have to supply the magic.

But it was tradition, and it was order. Addie might complain now. Okay, Addie might complain the whole time, but Brynn and Daisy would bounce and take immense joy in the parade. Then eat themselves silly at the various booths at the market.

They were why she did these things, and even a surly preteen wouldn't stop her from doing what needed to be done.

When Pen made it downstairs, Sadie was already in the kitchen, having seen to the milking with Dad. Brynn and Daisy were at the table eating cereal and coloring.

By the time Pen browbeat Addie downstairs, they were

running late. Pen snapped at least half a dozen times on the drive into town—at Dad for riling the girls up, at the girls for being riled up, at Sadie for not parking in the place they always parked in.

She was thoroughly disgusted with herself when they settled into a spot along the street—Dad veering off to talk to one of his friends, taking Addie with him. Brynn and Daisy bickered as they fought for space to sit on the curb. Pen bit her tongue to keep from scolding them and instead turned to Sadie.

"Were we that annoying?"

"I just bet." Sadie smiled her bland, helpful smile that Pen had learned to hate back when Sadie had come to stay with her after they'd lost Henry. Of course, Pen had always kept that to herself, lest her sister think her anger or irritation was grief.

She frowned. Maybe this whole feeling awful thing wasn't even all about Mom. Maybe it was just about…her.

Sadie touched her arm. "I can keep an eye on them if you need some time alone or—"

"Would you please stop treating me like I'm glass? I'm being a jerk. Treat me like I'm being a jerk."

Sadie looked at her with so much pity Pen wanted to scream.

"You've got a broken arm and you've had an emotional upheaval. You can have some jerk. So long as it's short-lived and not directed at your children. I'm a big girl. I can take it."

Which of course only served to make Pen feel worse. "I don't want you to take it. You shouldn't have to take it."

Sadie grinned. "Oh, well then. Stop being a jerk."

Pen laughed in spite of herself. Sadie had always been good about making her laugh. Pen hadn't seen it when she'd been younger, but after Henry had died Pen had realized how much Sadie had done for them all without ever really making a deal of it. She held Dad and the farm together.

Pen had left. For Henry. Sadie had stayed and kept it all together.

So, maybe this feeling inside of her wasn't grief. Maybe it was growing up—a second wave of maturity after the wave motherhood had given her. Maybe she was starting to see that her family and the people she loved were who they were regardless of her—her control, her help—and she had to see them as they were instead of how she wanted to twist their world to be.

"I hate Christmas," Pen muttered as the girls jostled each other while waiting for the parade to start. Not because she missed Mom or because of the stress of being the source of magic, but because she always seemed to look *inward* during Christmas. Looking inward inspired change and change was hard.

Really hard.

"You don't hate Christmas," Sadie replied easily. "You hate the stress, and I'm sure it's got more sadness for you than joy. I get that, but you don't hate *Christmas*."

Pen wasn't so sure, but she appreciated Sadie's attempt to

soothe her. Sadie was moving onto her tiptoes, trying to see over the much taller heads around her. "I should have made Colt come and put me on his shoulders," she muttered.

Pen smiled at the thought, at her little sister as this grown, wonderful woman. "Thank you."

Sadie turned to frown at her. "Huh?"

"You're a good sister. You grew up good. Without me."

Sadie rolled her eyes. "Please. I'd have been lost without you. You know it." Sadie wrapped her arm around Pen's waist. Pen knew the demonstrative move did not come naturally to her sister, so it made the gesture that much more special.

"I'll always need you," Sadie said, eyes straight ahead.

"I need you too." Which was not an easy admission, but easier with her sister's arm around her. Easier when Pen knew Sadie was pushing out of her comfort zone to give her some reassurances she needed.

The parade was starting farther down the street. Pen wouldn't be able to see anything yet, so she watched the girls, breathing through the aftermath of that admission to Sadie.

When she happened to look up, she locked gazes with Ethan across the street. He was in his uniform, and that gave her a bit of a jolt. Since he was a county deputy, he didn't always work Last Stand events, though usually the larger Christmas ones. She should have known she'd see him, at the very least.

He waved as if things were *normal*, then turned to talk to someone next to him.

Nothing was normal. Especially with him. And since she'd already made one admission, why not make another?

She kept her gaze on him. "I tried to kiss Ethan last night," she said quietly to Sadie.

She supposed that was half of her snapping this morning. No matter how many times she worked through it, she couldn't understand. She didn't want to share it with Sadie, who knew and loved them both. But apparently Sadie was all she had.

"Tried?" Sadie screeched, then looked around as a few heads turned their way. "What does tried mean?" she demanded on a whisper.

"I leaned in. He jumped away."

"Jumped?"

"Practically fell over himself to escape." Pen couldn't help but relive the moment. Over and over again. "I don't understand. You and Colt are together, so it's not like he's worried about Dad. If he wasn't interested, he would have let me down gently. So, I just don't get the dramatic run away."

"Did you ask him?"

"He ran away so fast he left smoke behind. Then he was already at work when I woke up this morning."

Sadie gave her a *really* look. "Pen."

"What?"

"Sure, he ran away, but since when don't you follow and demand answers?"

"I... You don't run after someone you try to kiss who rejects you."

Sadie shrugged. "Why not?"

"Because...because! It's embarrassing."

"Yeah, but you gotta live with the guy, so embarrassing or not, it's your life."

"Gee, thanks."

Sadie gave her a considering look. "Remember what you said to me when Colt and I were starting out. About not falling for him just because he was there and comfortable."

Pen remembered all too clearly. She hadn't exactly approved of Sadie and Colt starting something up. She wanted to believe it was because she'd been concerned about her sister's well-being, but looking back she thought maybe she'd been more selfishly concerned about change.

"Ethan *is* comfortable. But it's like you said about Colt. I don't feel the same way about Ethan as I do the other two. It's different. Besides, it was just a kiss." She glanced at the girls leaning forward to see the parade and lowered her voice. "Or an *attempt* at a kiss. I didn't go jump into bed with the guy, unlike *some* people."

Sadie rolled her eyes. "Okay, but it's complicated. Not just on your end. Those boys have a whole lot of complicated on their end."

"If Dad doesn't have a problem with you and Colt, how could he have a problem with me and Ethan?" Which was putting the cart before the horse considering *Ethan* was currently the one with the problem.

"That's what I'm saying. Ethan could have a million reasons not to kiss you even if he *is* interested. Maybe he made a promise to Mom. Maybe his childhood stuff warped him more than he lets on. There are a lot of reasons people hold back from what or who they might want. Colt has a whole legion of issues. Why wouldn't Ethan? Their families both sucked."

Pen looked for Ethan again, but he wasn't there anymore. Ethan always seemed so...solid and dependable. Not the kind of guy with issues. He didn't hide behind anything like Colt had hidden behind his jovial nature.

But she supposed people thought that about her too. Except she'd had a bunch of outward tragedies so people kind of expected her to be a mess. When she wasn't, they attributed it to being so strong or something.

But it was a lot of acting. Did Ethan have that kind of acting in him?

It'd be easier to think he just wasn't interested. It'd sting her pride some, but it wouldn't...hurt. The idea Ethan might have some awful or 'warped' reason for not wanting to kiss her made her sad for him.

"I think this belongs to you."

Pen turned toward Ethan's voice. Her mouth dropped at the fact he was leading Addie toward her. Addie had a mutinous expression on her face. "You aren't with Grandpa?"

"I believe she was trying to hitch a ride back to the farm."

"Adelaide Wakefield, have you lost your mind?" Pen demanded. *Hitch* a ride? Even though Pen knew most people in Last Stand, her daughter didn't. What a dangerous, stupid prank.

"I told you I didn't want to go to the stupid market!" Addie said. "And you won't even let me have a phone."

Pen didn't know what one had to do with the other, but it was better not to try and understand twelve-year-old logic.

"That does not give you the right to run away from your grandfather, to try and *hitch* a ride. My God what would your father think?"

"Nothing because he's *dead*," Addie spat. "I hate Christmas and you and everything!" She jerked away from Ethan's hand on her shoulder and darted into the crowd.

Pen was frozen for a moment. She thought Addie had been settling in. Oh, she was still moody, but it hadn't been as bad when they'd first moved and now...

"I could go talk to her," Ethan offered, as if nudging Pen to act.

"No, I should..." Pen let out a long breath. She was supposed to accept help, and if she talked to Addie right now she would most definitely lose her temper. "All right."

She noted his surprise, but he nodded and moved through the crowd in the direction Addie had gone.

"What was that all about?" Sadie asked gently.

"I don't even know." Exhausted didn't even begin to describe what Pen felt. "Watch these two. I better go tell Dad Ethan's got her."

CHRISTMAS FOR THE DEPUTY

ETHAN HAD NO idea why he'd offered to talk to Addie. He didn't know anything about dealing with angry girls.

But it had seemed better than sticking around while Pen looked both angry and hurt over her daughter, knowing he'd either have to comfort her or talk about last night. Knowing Pen, probably both.

The fuming pre-teen running through the crowd seemed a better choice all in all. Though she was running and he was walking, he closed the distance pretty easily—her blonde mop of hair a beacon to follow especially as she got farther away from the parade.

She headed straight for the playground and then plopped herself onto a swing. Ethan slowed his pace, giving her a few minutes to sit there and sulk. When he finally approached she glared at him.

The same glare Pen had given him last night.

"What do you want, tattletale?" she demanded.

Ethan stood there. He didn't even have to give her a censoring look before she wilted.

"Sorry," she muttered.

"That's okay. I did tattle."

She looked at him, considering. When he pointed to the swing next to her she shrugged. He positioned himself on the seat. It had been a long time since he'd been on a swing. It was not comfortable, but he worked to act casual.

"It wasn't a very nice thing to do, to scare your grandpa like that."

Tears filled her eyes but she screwed her face into an angry expression as if she could fight it away. She reminded him of Sadie and Mack and not of Pen at all, but he supposed Pen had that somewhere inside of her too. She just kept it locked down in a different way than her sisters.

Because she'd felt responsible. She'd had to be the one in control, and he knew that feeling all too well.

Maybe that's what Addie was struggling with. She was the oldest, after all.

"It's okay not to like things, but we all have to do things we don't like."

"No shit."

When Ethan raised both eyebrows, her cheeks went a shade of red. "Uncle Colt says it."

"I don't think that excuse would fly with your mama."

"She doesn't care about me."

"I'll let you get away with saying a lot, but not that. Because we both know that isn't true."

"I didn't want to move here! She said I would learn to like it and I don't. I hate it. I hate my class. I hate my teacher. I hate all these stupid Christmas things. I'm never going to like it. Ever."

How hard was it to validate her feelings while also validating Pen's? "I know you feel that way. And you have every right to. But I know your mom pretty well, and I know even if it doesn't feel like it, she's doing what she thinks will be the best for you."

"It isn't best!"

"Sometimes..." He didn't want to say all adults knew best since he knew that was a lie. "Sometimes what's best doesn't feel good in the moment, because change is really hard. And you've had to deal with a lot of unfair change, Addie. You don't have to be happy about it."

"Well, I'm not."

Ethan blew out a breath. He'd known this wasn't going to be easy but he didn't know what to do. How to fix it.

He thought about Susannah, who'd been the only one in his childhood who'd ever tried to fix anything for him. "You know, I used to run away from home."

Addie gave him a sideways glance, suddenly interested and trying desperately not to be.

"For different reasons, I didn't like my home very much. When I was a little older than you I started trying to get in trouble, because I thought if I got in enough trouble I wouldn't have to live at home anymore."

Now he had her full attention, and he hoped to God she didn't try to start getting into trouble like he had. If he had to admit to Pen he'd put *that* idea in her head, he was so screwed.

"One time, your grandma found me doing something bad."

"What were you doing?"

"Uh-uh. I'm not giving you any ideas, girlie."

She wrinkled her nose, but didn't press, so he kept going.

"She let me off with a warning, so then I started calling her names. Because I thought she'd get mad and I wouldn't have to go home. After a little while, she got real close. She looked me right in the eye, and she asked me why I didn't want to go home."

The memory made his throat tighten, but he cleared it and looked over at Addie. She wasn't the picture-perfect image of Pen like Daisy was. She looked more like Henry all in all. But she was watching him with big hazel eyes that reminded him an awful lot of Susannah.

And Susannah was why he was here. "You know what I did when she asked me that?"

Addie shook her head.

"I started crying."

Addie's eyes widened. "You *cried?*"

Ethan nodded. "Sure did. And boy was I embarrassed. But no one had ever asked me that before. I'd never expected anyone to listen. But she did and she helped me. Even though she didn't know me or love me yet."

Addie looked down at her feet.

"So, I know it's hard. I know it's hard to not want to be where you're stuck, but so many people love you. That's a really lucky thing to have. And maybe if you talked to them about it without being nasty, they might be able to help you find ways to like it."

"I don't want to like it," she grumbled, kicking at the ground.

"That might be your first problem."

She scowled, but when Ethan stood she slid off her swing and stood too.

"Ready to go back?"

She shrugged, which he took as a yes. He started walking back toward the parade, but before they got back into the crowd, Addie slid her hand into his.

He looked down at the small hand, dwarfed by his much larger one. She had chipped pink polish on her nails, and a bracelet made up of delicate plastic roses.

And she held his hand and walked with him back to her family.

Damn.

Chapter Eight

"MOM, YOU ALREADY put in the salt."

Pen blinked down at Brynn who was standing on a chair helping her make sugar cookies, just like Pen had done when she was Brynn's age.

Pen liked to think she'd listened a little better to her mother's instructions than Brynn usually did, but who knew? Pen wasn't listening very well right now because she kept looking out the window over the sink to see if she could catch a glimpse of Ethan's headlights.

Pen was starting to wonder if sitting around waiting for Ethan to show up so she could talk to him was going to be her lot in life. It didn't seem so bad. What did seem bad was the fact Addie had refused to tell her what she'd talked to Ethan about this morning before he'd brought her back to the parade.

Addie had still been sulky the rest of the market, but she hadn't tried to bolt again.

Her little girl had tried to run away. *Hitch* a ride. It made all Pen's silly fears about not making the right cookies and being a failure seem…actually silly.

Who cared about cookies or how much she was like her

mother if her daughter was trying to escape?

Pen swallowed at the now-familiar panic in her throat. Once Ethan got home from work and told her what Addie had said she'd be able to chill. Once he told her... How. How?

"Mom?"

Pen forced herself to focus on Brynn and the cookies. One step at a time. That was how anyone got through life. "Okay, so we already did the salt. What else do we need to do?"

She worked with Brynn, trying to be more present and patient as they finished mixing the dough. They'd chill it overnight then spend Sunday morning cutting them out and decorating and...

Oh, damn it, where on earth was Ethan?

Pen looked down at Brynn who was trying to sneak some dough without Pen seeing. "Brynnie... Do you know what was wrong with Addie this morning?"

Brynn smiled brightly, a mischievous glint to her eye Pen swore she'd been born with. "She's a butt?" Brynn said sweetly.

Pen sighed. "Not what I meant and you know it, young lady. I'll put this in the fridge. Why don't you go check on how Grandpa is doing with the tree?"

"He was swearing last time I checked."

"Well, if he's still swearing, I'll go get Colt to help him with it."

Brynn hopped off the chair, sticking a big wad of dough

she'd 'hidden' in her hand into her mouth as she bounced out of the kitchen.

Oh, that girl was going to be the kind of teenage trouble Pen didn't know how she'd weather.

She heard the faint sound of an engine and lunged toward the window. Headlights. She assumed they were Ethan's since if Colt or Sadie came over they'd use their farm utility vehicle or one of Colt's new horses.

She grabbed her coat and wrapped it around her as she moved through the mudroom and out to the back porch.

Ethan was already stepping out of his truck. He'd changed out of his uniform, but he still wore his cowboy hat. When he noticed her on the porch he stopped on a dime, and looked back at his vehicle. Like he was considering getting back in and turning right around.

She almost found it amusing, but she needed to talk to him about Addie.

First, anyway.

"I want to talk to you about Addie," she announced, since she figured he'd bolt if he thought she was going to bring up the kiss attempt.

"Okay," he replied, finally moving forward.

"What did you two talk about this morning?"

"Why?"

Pen fisted her good hand on her hip. "What do you mean why? She's my daughter."

"She's a person. I figure she should probably tell you herself."

"Well, you figure wrong. She said you didn't talk about anything, but she came back and didn't try to run away again or fight with me. So, I want to know what you did." *How you reached that girl when I can't seem to.* "She should talk to me." Pen hadn't meant to say that last part since it sounded childish even to her, but there it was. Because it was so annoyingly easy to announce her flaws to Ethan.

"Shouldn't she talk to anyone who will listen to her?"

Pen let herself sink onto the stair—exactly the same spot she'd been sitting last night. "Why are you being reasonable?" she asked miserably. Of *course* she wanted her daughter to talk to whomever she needed to talk to. Pen just didn't know when it had turned into not being her.

He did not sit next to her, but he smiled down at her. "I figure someone has to be reasonable around here."

She looked up at him. "Well, guess what? It's not going to be the mom."

He smiled, and it wasn't the *cop* smile. No, this was warmer. Like he enjoyed her less reasonable, less controlled thoughts. It was the kind of smile that eased some of the pressure in her lungs.

"That's fair enough," he said quietly.

It was her first instinct to stop talking, even though she knew she needed to talk. To let it out. And being with Ethan in the dark made leaning into what she knew she needed to do a lot easier than if it had been Sadie or Dad. "I thought it was getting better for her. I thought..."

He heaved out a sigh then sat next to her. She knew he

didn't want to, because of last night, but he did it anyway.

It was…nice to have that. She might be learning to lean on the people she'd spent her whole life trying to protect and take care of, but it was nice to be able to do it with someone she'd never felt beholden to.

"It's a hard change. I moved into this house when I was a little older than Addie. I hated where I came from. I never ever wanted to go back there. And still some days it'd hit me out of the blue… I didn't want *this* place. I didn't want *your* family. I wanted my own."

Knowing what she knew about Ethan's family she couldn't understand why. "You really felt that way?"

"Never for long. And it stopped eventually. It wasn't a rational feeling, but it was there. The thing is, the things that are *good* for you don't always feel good. That's basically what I told Addie this morning. And that you loved her and were just trying to do what was best."

"I believed that when I made the decision to move home."

He patted her hand. "You should keep believing it. There's no better place to grow up than right here, with your father and the goats. Of that I'm sure."

"Can you remind me of that every now and again?"

He patted her hand again. "You got it. We've got your back. And theirs."

His hand rested over hers as if he'd forgotten all about last night.

But she hadn't. Because one of the many things

parenthood taught you was how to multitask dealing with your worries and concerns and the things you couldn't make sense of no matter how hard you tried.

She turned her hand under his, making them palm to palm. He stared at their hands like he didn't understand what had happened. But he didn't jump away. Slowly, she lifted her gaze to his.

He was handsome, always had been, but the more she understood he was...complicated, the more she wanted to study it. The sharp jaw and firm mouth, and the way no matter how careful he was, certain emotions always popped up in his eyes.

His hand was warm and rough. He was a *good* man, no matter what complications he hid under all that quiet sturdiness. The kind of man who'd sit down next to her even when she made him uncomfortable.

If she was a good person, she'd probably stop trying to make him uncomfortable. Except, no. No. Discomfort wasn't always bad. She didn't *enjoy* that panic attack she'd had the other day, but it had unlocked some of the ways she'd been denying what she was really feeling.

Ethan definitely needed to unlock some things.

"You've got my back, but if I tried to kiss you again, you'd run right out of here."

He removed his hand and immediately rose to his feet.

She looked up at his retreating back with the most regal expression she could muster. "You surprise me, Ethan."

She got the reaction out of him that she wanted. He

stopped walking away and looked at her like she'd lost her mind.

"Was I not clear enough last night?" he replied, and his voice was calm but his eyes were *not*, and wasn't that fascinating. There was something here. Something that made her feel...

Like herself. Not the woman who had to keep everything under control and make everything okay. Just Penelope.

And *nothing* about the way Ethan was acting was *clear*. "No, sorry. Acting like a scared beaten puppy scrambling away from someone trying to pet him is *not* clear. You've surely faced scarier things than me trying to kiss you."

"I wouldn't be so sure," he muttered. Then he squared his shoulders, and held her gaze. "I'm not interested," he said firmly, sharply even.

She laughed, couldn't help it. Oh, she knew he was serious, but that didn't make it *true*. Slowly, she got to her feet. "Maybe you're a good liar after all, Ethan. I wish I could believe it, but no matter what you *say* I know you well enough. If you weren't interested, you could have told me that without bolting last night. I, in fact, have no doubt you would have done everything in your power to let me down gently. So gently I would hardly have known you'd done it."

His expression scrunched together into confusion. "You surprised me."

"Oh, *please*."

"Listen. You've had a rough go these past few months...years. It's been hard and—"

"Oh. Gee. Thanks for pointing it out. Is this where you tell me my personal tragedy made me too stupid to know what I'm doing? Because that's beneath you."

"You shouldn't—"

She didn't want to get angry about this, but he was making it difficult. "*You* shouldn't tell *me* what to do. I'm not asking about *me*, Ethan. I know what I feel. Maybe you think less of me because I haven't been keeping it all locked down lately, but—"

"That isn't what I said," he snapped sharply. So sharply she did in fact stop talking. "Don't put words in my mouth. I will not tolerate that."

She believed him. On that, she believed him. He held himself tense, but he didn't walk away. Not yet. So, she continued.

"I know that if you weren't interested you would let me down gently. Not act like a wounded bird."

"I thought I was an abused puppy."

"Both work." Maybe on more than one level. She should be easier on him. She shouldn't push him when he had his own things to work out.

But wasn't *pushing* what fixed things?

"I'm just looking for an answer, Ethan. A real, truthful answer about why you ran away."

"I told you, I'm not interested."

"A lie is not an answer." She held his gaze for a moment more and then decided when it came to that stubborn expression on his face, retreat was the best course of action.

For today.

She swept by him. "You just let me know when you're ready to give me the truth. I can wait."

She stepped inside, grinning when she heard him swearing under his breath.

ETHAN ATE BREAKFAST at the Martin table the next morning out of sheer stubbornness. He was going to handle Pen. Mostly because if he didn't she'd just keep thinking things she shouldn't be thinking.

Pen acted like she always did. Well, maybe not always. She was a little...louder. More *determinedly* cheerful. A little bit like she was being jovial *at* him.

Let her be. He had no plans to give her a truthful answer to her pointless question. Eventually she'd believe he really wasn't interested.

Hopefully.

He glanced across the table. Brynn had already eaten and ran out to the goat barn with Fritz and Sadie, and Addie hadn't shown up yet. But Daisy sat there, watching him solemnly while she ate her cereal.

No, she wasn't watching him. She was staring at the badge-shaped patch on his chest.

Which made him feel like a tool. He tried not to be in uniform too much around the girls, though in the past six months he had been on occasion. They'd never really acted like they'd noticed or cared before, but he should have thought this through. He'd just been thinking if Pen pressed, he could leave for work immediately.

He should have thought about the girls. Eating a meal in his uniform would feel different to them than just stopping by in it. It would feel domestic and be a reminder of…everything bad that had happened in their lives.

"You done, sweet pea?" Pen asked into the quiet.

Daisy nodded and handed her bowl to Pen. Pen turned back to doing the dishes. She'd already had an argument with Sadie about doing them, but Pen argued loading the dishwasher one-handed was hardly a challenge.

She made it look easy, he'd give her that. He pushed his chair back, ready to stand and leave before Daisy darted off and left him and Pen alone in the kitchen. Before he could feel worse about trying to prove a point to Pen and ending up hurting Daisy.

But Daisy walked right over to him before he stood. After one solemn look she crawled up onto his leg and situated herself there. She reached out and traced the patch on his arm, then the one on his chest.

He brushed his hand over the top of her head, heart about cracking in two. Then he settled his arm around her to keep her balanced on his leg. "Does it bother you?" he asked softly.

"Daddy used to wear one like that," she said, as if working through some great problem.

But there was no problem here. No more uniform in the

house. He could change at work, or even at his apartment. He still had a key through December. "I know, sweetheart. Listen, if it bothers you I won't wear it inside the—"

"I like it," she said resolutely. She looked up at him, and this close he could see all the differences between Pen and her youngest. Her hair was a few shades lighter than Pen's, though it would likely darken as she got older. Her face was rounder, another thing that might change. So much future change.

She'd get older. Grow up and life would be cruel and that just didn't seem fair.

He was pulled out of that reverie by Daisy sliding off his leg. He sat there for he wasn't sure how long, Daisy still staring at him, and him feeling like there was some great weight on his chest.

Finally, he cleared his throat and stood. "I need to get going to work."

Daisy nodded thoughtfully. Then she motioned him to bend down with one finger. For a second he could picture her as an adult doing that to some *boy* he'd have to dismember. Piece by piece. Enthusiastically.

He bent over as she bade. She gave him a prim kiss on the cheek. Then she smiled and skipped out the door, presumably to find Brynn and Fritz with the goats.

Ethan had to hold on to the back of the chair to keep from keeling over. "Your kids are killing me," he managed to croak.

When he looked up at Pen, she was smiling. "I'd feel

bad, but I'm enjoying it too much."

Some of that awful pressure Daisy had left him with eased. "My pain *amuses* you?"

"Sort of. You're not really in pain, Ethan. You like it." She slid a dish into the bottom rack of the dishwasher. "You're just afraid to like it."

Somehow those words were worse than Daisy being so sweet to him. Because they felt a little too close to the truth. How *much* he liked all of this.

Which was a painful realization. One he didn't want, because it made his life harder and he'd worked for years to make his life easy. Simple.

"Maybe I don't want to be runner-up to your dead husband and their dead father."

Pain had always made him mean. It was why he avoided it best he could. He didn't like that black wave of guilt after being mean. Didn't like the ways it reminded him of his father.

Pen didn't wilt or even look hurt. She smiled. "Took you all night to come up with that one, huh?" She shook her head. "I don't think you really think that, but to be clear, when I look at you in uniform I don't see Henry. I see you. I didn't look at Henry in his uniform and see you. Or my mother. All three of you were a type, that's for sure, but you're hardly the same three people."

Ethan didn't have the words, because all that seemed to bubble up inside of him was an apology. He wasn't going to apologize to her. Not while she was pushing at him this way.

Making things painful this way.

"I loved my husband, you know that. I also have three daughters I love. Two sisters. One doesn't replace the other, or get some bigger piece of all that love."

"You don't love me."

"Of course I do. I love all three of you boys. But what I feel for Colt and Bracken is different, has always been different, than what I felt for you. Maybe it's romantic love. Maybe it isn't. But both of us would have to be brave enough to figure that out."

"No." God, no. It wasn't a question of bravery. It was a question of sanity. Of keeping things the way they were, where no one got hurt. No one felt too much and had it blow up in their face.

He shook his head. Because bigger than that emotional mess, there was the far more important thing. He had to protect her and the girls. From everything a larger connection to him would bring.

That was what he had to remember. His father was what he was scared of...not hurt and emotions. Those were best left alone.

She closed the dishwasher door with a flourish, and though irritation snapped in her expression, her voice was mild. "Then you'll have to think up a new excuse I guess."

Much like last night, she sailed out of the room leaving him...lost. And alone.

Chapter Nine

PEN WAS DETERMINED to enjoy the annual tree lighting in front of the library in Last Stand. Sure, it was cold. And yes, too many people were bustled together. But they were people she knew, people she'd grown up with. People who'd brought casseroles after Mom had died, who'd sent cards after Henry.

Her daughters' teachers, and the business owners and committee members who kept things like this tree lighting going, year after year.

She really was happy to be home. It hadn't happened overnight, no matter what she'd told herself. There'd been a relief at moving back to Last Stand, but she'd spent her entire adult life in San Antonio. No matter how she'd kept herself busy these past few months trying to take care of everyone and make sure everything was just *so*, she hadn't felt right and settled.

It probably had a lot to do with the Mom stuff she was still working through, and maybe even to a certain extent Henry stuff. She'd moved on best she could, accepted he was gone, but leaving the house they'd made together was another step in that.

She'd convinced herself she was *healed* and refused to acknowledge that her choice to move home hadn't been 100 percent perfect and happy making.

Because life was a heck of a lot more complicated than she wanted to admit. But the more she admitted it to herself, the happier she felt.

The big tree suddenly glowed with light. Daisy's squeal made Pen smile, and even Addie clapped with the crowd.

Yes, she was happy to be home in Last Stand. Happy to be surrounded by her family.

Daisy tapped her on the shoulder. Daisy didn't say anything, just pointed to Ethan in the distance.

"Ethan's working, sweet pea. We'll go say hi in a little bit."

Addie stood on her tiptoes trying to see over the crowd. "We should buy him a cookie or some hot chocolate. It's cold."

"Hot chocolate? I want hot chocolate!" Brynn announced, bouncing.

"My treat," Colt offered, lifting Brynn up onto his shoulders, which was possibly her favorite spot in the world. "Come on, girls. Follow me."

"Didn't you say you wanted to go buy some ornaments for the girls' stockings?" Sadie asked in a whisper when Pen fell into step behind Colt. "We'll take care of the girls. You go get some shopping done."

"Oh. Well…" Pen looked around at the booths for the Christkindlmarkt. She hadn't been able to do any shopping the other day because everyone had been together. Now would be a good time to get a few things she wasn't going to order online.

"Whatever you buy, just hand it over to Ethan," Sadie continued, stopping as Colt kept moving forward with the girls. "He gets off at eight. He'll bring them home in his patrol car, then you can hide them after the girls go to bed."

"My, you think of everything, don't you?"

Sadie grinned. "Always. Now, shoo. We'll keep the girls busy."

"Well, all right." Pen felt a bit unmoored since this wasn't part of the plan, but she supposed she had to get used to being a little more spontaneous. Maybe it would be good for her.

She was surprised to find…it was. She shopped and talked with people she'd known in high school. She ran into Brynn's teacher and had a quick conversation about how well Brynn was doing and her interest in helping out in the classroom.

She bought the girls ornaments, and herself a hot chocolate and some stollen. She rarely got it because the girls didn't like it, so they were usually splitting lebkuchen cookies.

She found herself back at the Christmas tree, watching the lights twinkle in the cold evening. It was quieter over here, though people walked by chatting and laughing with each other.

Pen couldn't remember the last time she'd gone out and

done something on her own. Oh, the grocery store now and then, or a trip to the pharmacy. But she hadn't gone to a movie made for adults since long before Henry had died. She hadn't had a shopping trip to herself that wasn't harried or specifically geared toward a list in just as long.

She hadn't even thought about getting a job—life was a constant balancing act and she and the girls had been financially well taken care of after Henry's death. She helped out at the farm, and would help even more once the tourist side of things opened up. But it was all…connected.

Maybe she'd do more of this. Get out on her own. Sadie and Colt and Dad were busy with the farm and opening it to guests and adding Colt's cattle, but they could work together to watch the girls an hour every few weeks so Pen could just…have a few moments to remember who she was beyond *Mom*.

She hadn't thought she wanted that. Being Mom was a safe place not because she was actually safe or didn't worry, but because she always had things to *do*. If she didn't know how to help Addie, she knew how to fold laundry. If she didn't know how to help Daisy with her reading struggles, she at least knew how to help Brynn with her math homework.

She had a clear role. Mom. Protector. Fighter.

Walking through the booths at the Christmas market in Last Stand, Texas, staring up at the tree she'd watched light up every December almost every year of her life, all she had to be was Penelope Martin-Wakefield.

Whoever that was.

Definitely a scary thing to try and figure out, but...exciting too. Hopeful.

Somewhere people were singing 'God Rest Ye Merry Gentlemen' and Pen smiled up at the tree. She would cling to hopeful. Maybe she'd even embrace change.

She'd try, anyway.

Her phone buzzed. "Sadie? Everything all right?"

"Just great!" Sadie said, far too cheerfully. "Hey, um, just FYI, we took the girls home."

"What?"

"They were tired and you were talking with someone. I figured we'd take them home and you could stay and enjoy yourself."

"How am *I* supposed to get home?" Pen demanded, not trusting the overly casual note to Sadie's voice.

"Like I said, Ethan gets off at eight. He can drive you home."

Ethan. Pen turned around. He was tall and in uniform, including his cowboy hat, so he was easy to spot, even in the crowd.

"Does Ethan know he's in charge of driving me home?" Pen asked, watching as Ethan talked to a younger couple Pen didn't recognize.

When her sister didn't respond, Pen scowled at the phone. "Sadie," she growled in a warning voice.

"Colt will handle that. Do some Christmas shopping. Enjoy a coffee or a drink by yourself. Just...take a break."

"I don't take breaks."

"I've noticed. *Dad* has noticed. Christmas is stressful. De-stress."

Which she had been doing, hadn't she? Doing and enjoying. "All right." She pushed out a breath. "All right."

"Great. See you in a bit."

Pen hung up her phone and watched Ethan. He said goodbye to the couple then pulled his phone out of his pocket. He scowled at the screen, which she presumed meant Colt had texted him that he was in charge of bringing her home.

He looked up and scanned the crowd, slowly softening the scowl on his face to something neutral. Interesting to watch him do that while he didn't know she was looking. Eventually his gaze made its way over to the tree and finally landed on her.

She smiled and shrugged.

He started making his way toward her, and she decided to wait. She sipped her hot chocolate and watched the tree as someone waylaid Ethan. Once he'd taken care of whatever they wanted he finally arrived.

"I'm working," he announced, and he sounded pleasant all in all, but she knew he was irritated despite him giving no outward signs. Something about the way he held his shoulders.

"Yes, of course," she agreed. "Hard at work taming this dangerous crowd." She gestured toward the ever-diminishing group of people. Happy and jovial with absolutely no threat of anything otherwise.

"I'm glad it's a joke, but—"

"It's not a joke. But I also know you can walk around with me without breaking any precious policy. If you get a call, you'll go to it. If you don't, I buy you a hot chocolate."

"Is Sadie...up to something?" he asked, studying her.

She knew what he meant, but refused to bite if he wasn't going to be specific. "What would she be up to, Ethan?" She smiled innocently at him until he frowned.

"Fine," he muttered. "But a lebkuchen better come with that hot chocolate." His obvious attempt to sound grumpy failed, and amused her greatly.

"Of course," she returned with mock gravity. She fell into step next to him, heading back toward the market.

She might not be certain who Penelope Martin-Wakefield was outside of 'mother,' but she knew she wanted it to have *something* to do with this man next to her.

ETHAN WALKED AROUND the market with Pen. He kept wishing a call would come in that would necessitate him leaving the premises, but of course all was quiet.

It was stupid to feel on display, as if walking about town with Pen *meant* something. He would have done the same if she was here with the girls, or if it had only been Fritz. Him walking around with a Martin, any Martin, was as common as anything else.

It felt all…wrong now. Obvious. Like there was a spotlight on them.

Which worried him only because of his father, not because of the riot of *feelings* jangling inside of his gut like a parade.

"Shouldn't you be wearing your sling?"

"I hate that thing. And everyone looks at it and wonders what happened and I'm tired of telling the story. If I keep my sleeve over the cast I can minimize most of the curiosity."

"How did you end up alone and needing a ride back to the farm?" he asked, going for casual and failing. Miserably.

Pen only smiled that knowing smile at him and then answered honestly. "Sadie was sneaky. She said she was going to watch the girls while I did some Christmas shopping. Then she took them home instead. She said she wanted to give me a break. Which is the last thing I thought I needed, but it was nice."

"Well, I'm glad."

"But not glad about having to take me home."

"I'm going there anyway," he replied doing his best to keep his shoulders relaxed and his expression mild.

She shook her head and chuckled. "You know, it's funny. Becoming an adult away from home then coming back. You and Colt aren't what I thought you were."

"Don't you mean who?"

"No. You're both extraordinarily good men with good hearts. That'll always be true and I've always known it. *Who* you are won't change. But what you are? I thought Colt was

Mr. Have-A-Good-Time without a care in the world. And I thought you were just naturally quiet and stoic."

"I am naturally quiet and stoic."

She laughed and Ethan tried not to notice a few heads turning to watch them with speculative eyes. That kind of rumor was the last thing he needed.

"You're a *storm*, Ethan."

He stared down at her, stopping in his tracks, which led a few people walking behind him to grumble.

Again, Pen just laughed then led them up to the booth that was selling hot chocolate and a variety of German Christmas treats. Pen got him a hot chocolate and a cookie and when she handed them to him, he could only stare for a second before he gathered his wits.

Pen gave him a speculative look as he finally took the outstretched offerings. He cleared his throat and moved out of the line. "Your mom did this with me once."

"We always came."

"No, just me. Before she moved me in. I'd stolen some beer from the saloon's booth and she was on duty and caught me."

"No matter how hard I try I can't picture you as a little bad boy. Colt's easy to believe. You? I just can't."

"I didn't particularly want to be bad. I wanted to escape. And instead of arresting me or even lecturing me, she had me return the beer. Then she brought me to a booth and bought me a hot chocolate and a cookie."

Pen smiled up at him as they walked down the line of

booths. "That's a nice memory."

"All of mine with her are."

Pen laughed sadly. "Well, you're lucky. Too often I remember butting heads with her. Arguing and yelling and being a little brat."

"That doesn't sound like Addie at all," Ethan replied with a grin.

"I wasn't that bad."

"Oh, but you were."

She gave him a teasing slap across the arm holding the cookie. He ate half then offered her the other knowing her affinity for sweets. She took it without hesitation.

"It's the age, I think, having watched all you girls go through it," Ethan offered. "And now Addie. You lash out against the ones you love because you have all that teenage angst, and the people you love won't toss you out."

"Addie's only twelve."

"She's had a tough twelve."

"Yeah, she has."

They walked back to the now lit Christmas tree. He didn't have too much longer before his shift was over and he found himself wishing for more time like this. Being able to walk and talk with each other without complication. Because here his uniform and badge stood in the way. It was that barrier he needed between them.

Once they went back to the farm it would be all confused again. Difficult. For him. She seemed so…serene all of a sudden he had to wonder if she'd found some magic *answer* to everything.

"I guess Sadie knew what she was doing. You seem happier."

"I'm getting there." She smiled at the tree and took a deep breath. "I had to let go of some things. Like thinking I could ever make life *easy*. I kept thinking the right sequence of moves would make things uncomplicated. Permanently nice. But that's silly. I don't think there's been an easy thing in my life since I gave birth to Addie. Motherhood isn't easy, even when it's amazing."

"I don't know how you do it."

"You're great with them. It can't be that much of a mystery."

"Sure, but they aren't my responsibility. I don't have to be the center of their world. I can stay on the periphery where it's…"

"Easy?" She studied him, but it felt like a trick question.

But it was exactly the truth. If you kept a certain distance between yourself and everyone else things *were* easier. He'd had a lot of hard in his life. He deserved easy.

So did she, for that matter, but kids complicated that.

More importantly though, easy kept everyone safe. You put up enough walls the bad parts of him couldn't climb them and hurt the people he loved.

"As much as I wish for easy, it isn't… The best things in life aren't. They can be simple, but they're never easy. Because caring about someone that way isn't ever easy, but what's as fulfilling as my daughter looking up to me?"

She stood there in the glow of the tree lights, bags hooked on one arm, her cast hidden under the sleeve of her other arm. She reminded him more of the girl he'd known. She'd always been…well, Pen. Organized and on top of everything and with a certain weight on her shoulders she herself placed there. But there'd been a raggedness to that since Henry died.

She was letting that go, little by little.

And what are you doing?

A good question. One he didn't particularly want to answer when she turned and smiled at him.

He could not give in to this *thing* between them. He had good reasons. The kind of reasons that would keep her and her girls safe. They shouldn't *dim* in the face of that smile, they should intensify.

"I have to radio out."

Pen nodded. Because she understood his job in a way a lot of people didn't. Even Fritz got a little grumpy about certain parts of it, and Ethan didn't know if it stemmed from being reminded of Susannah, or having so much time pass since Susannah was a police officer that he'd simply forgotten what the job required of a person.

But Pen had lived with a police officer for most of her life. She knew.

Which didn't *matter*. Not to him. He radioed out, then turned back to her. She was watching him with that careful consideration he knew better than to ask about.

"I'm parked over at the PD," he said pointing in that

direction. She fell into step behind him, a heavy quiet enveloping them. She seemed fine with it, but it was making him...edgy.

"I usually change at my apartment, but the girls really don't seem to mind."

"They didn't see Henry much in his uniform. He didn't have a take-home car. And the Texas Ranger dress code is different than a uniform. Simplistic, but I think it helps. I also think they're young enough they don't quite equate the career to the...end."

"It doesn't bother you?"

She shook her head. "I think the fact that Mom died of cancer, and Henry died in the line of duty... I don't know. Death happens, no matter what you wear or who you are. It doesn't mean I don't worry. It just means the uniform doesn't symbolize what happened to Henry for me. I've loved too many cops for that to happen."

Loved. That word was really starting to get annoying. Pen said it to the girls all the time. So did Fritz. Sadie and Colt were forever saying goodbye for the ten seconds they'd be apart with kisses and I love yous.

Love was too complicated to talk about, even if you felt it. Because of course he loved his brothers, and Fritz. He loved those girls because they were...they were...lovable. He loved the Martin girls—women—because even though they didn't feel like sisters the way his biological one had, they were still family.

But he didn't need to say it. Examine it.

Ethan had said I love you to one person in his entire life, and he didn't plan on that changing anytime soon. Susannah had died and it had seemed a good enough time to let that saying die with her.

Why his brain was taking *that* particular detour was so far beyond him he didn't even know how to rationalize it to himself.

They got into his car and drove home. They chatted about shopping she still needed to do and when Mack and Bracken were going to come home, and they settled into easy periods of silence as well.

When he pulled up in front of the Martin house, lit up to the nines in red, green and white, he felt for sure there was something he should say, but no words came.

They both got out of the car. Pen grabbed her bags and began to head inside. Before she reached the porch she turned around, looking up at the bright half-moon shining above them. She stood there for a moment, bathed in moonlight, and all he could do was stare.

This had to stop. Time alone with Pen. There was no reason for it. All it did was make him ache for something he couldn't allow himself. So, it had to stop.

But when she stepped forward to him, he didn't back away. He didn't tell her to stop. He stood there as she stood on her tiptoes and wrapped an arm around him and gave a friendly squeeze.

"Thanks for the drive home. I know you didn't want to, but I really needed tonight in a way I didn't realize." She reached out and he tensed, but he was a police officer trained to defuse dangerous situations.

Or, in the case of anything to do with Pen, he stood perfectly still and hoped it would go away.

She let her hand slide down his arm as she went back to flat-footed, but she stood exactly there. Too close. Too…

"Aren't you going to run away?" she asked in a quiet voice, humor making the ends of her mouth curve.

He should. He should run in the opposite direction. His limbs weren't listening. They tightened around her of their own accord—it had to be that they were in charge here because he absolutely knew he shouldn't.

He never took what he couldn't or shouldn't have. Not anymore. He'd made promises to himself. Over and over again.

But all those words jumbled in his head. Things that had always been warnings and rebuttals started to sound like encouragement. When she did nothing but stand there, too close and far too beautiful, it seemed the only thing to do.

Break every promise he'd ever made to himself about her. Every other possibility disappeared so that there was only this and her.

His mouth touching hers, his arm wrapping around her waist and pulling her close. Every part of him that he kept locked down and away springing to life.

He'd initiated it—he knew he had. But why or *how* or what on earth had possessed him was beyond him. And didn't seem to matter with his lips on hers.

It wasn't what he'd imagined or dreamed it would be on those rare times his subconscious got the better of him. Because he'd never felt anything like *this*, not even in a dream. There was no way to explain it. Something inside of him that grew—something outside of him that brightened every dark thought he'd ever had.

Whatever he'd thought a kiss could be wasn't this. She tasted like sugar and was warm against a cold Texas winter night. And she kissed him back, like they'd been made to do only this. Forever.

She lifted her arm, as if to pull him closer, but the bag she had hanging off of it banged into them and she startled away. She blinked up at him as if waking up from a dream.

Could they pretend it had been?

"We shouldn't have…" He couldn't finish the sentence. Shouldn't have? He couldn't survive this and yet *shouldn't have* felt all wrong.

But her expression made something like fear bolt through him. Because she looked pale. Shaken. Not in a good way.

"I think you're right," she finally said. "We shouldn't have."

Which made no sense. At all. She was the one pursuing this. She was the one…

"Wait." He nearly held on to her as she moved away. Even though he wanted her away. But since when did *she* want away? "What?"

"I have to go," she said, already turning around and

striding purposefully for the door.

"What?"

But she didn't answer. She disappeared inside. And he...

What?

Chapter Ten

"There you are," Sadie greeted cheerfully. She was the only one in the kitchen, thank God. "The girls and Dad—"

"I'm just going to go hide this stuff," Pen managed to choke out as she hurried up the stairs. She got to her room and shut the door and then simply sank onto the floor and sobbed.

The well of emotion was so broad and deep she didn't have a word for it. Part grief, part surprise, and a big, huge part of it fear.

She'd thought she knew what she was doing when it came to Ethan, but that kiss... It was bigger than anything she'd imagined or even expected. Too big. Too much.

She'd loved her husband with everything she was, and she never thought she could feel that again. She'd been happy to believe moving on would mean feeling something for someone, even love, but nothing so big and all-encompassing. Because how could you feel it twice in one lifetime with two different people?

But that kiss had been something closer to magic than she'd realized existed. It had made her forget everything. It had filled her up with so many emotions, she'd *had* to run away.

The knock that eventually came wasn't exactly unexpected. "Pen?" Sadie said quietly.

Pen tried to wipe at her face, but it was pointless. Sadie wouldn't understand this. Heck, Pen wasn't even sure *she* understood it.

But Sadie would listen, and maybe Pen didn't need her to understand. Maybe she just needed to unburden herself.

Pen opened the door from her position on the floor. When Sadie stepped in she immediately sank to her knees in front of Pen.

"What's wrong?"

"I'm okay. Nothing is wrong." Not wrong exactly anyway. Just confusing.

At Sadie's disapproving look, Pen managed a smile. "Really. I don't know how to explain... I..." Too many words and emotions jangled inside of her, so she went with the simplest explanation even though it wouldn't make sense. "Ethan kissed me."

Sadie closed the door and moved from her knees in front of Sadie to a seat next to Pen on the floor. "I thought that's what you wanted," Sadie said gently.

"I did. I do." It wasn't that she wanted to take it back. Well, part of her did. The scared part. But it was more than that.

"So? Was he a jerk? I'll knock his teeth out." Sadie waved her fist, then seemed to consider the size of it. "Or have Colt do it. He might if Ethan was a jerk to you."

"No." Pen laughed. "No. It was a great kiss. It was… I hadn't thought it through. I hadn't… I haven't kissed anyone since Henry died. I didn't think that would matter, but…"

"Oh."

Pen wanted to laugh because that *oh* wasn't an *I understand*. It was an *I don't know what to say to that*. But Sadie was sitting here. Sadie who tended to avoid emotional confrontation was sitting next to her letting her cry and be confusing. Offering comfort.

Sadie had changed this past year. Matured maybe, or just allowed herself to open up more fully. In part because she'd fallen in love with Colt, and love was big enough to change a person. Make them better or worse.

"I'm not sad or mad or hurt," Pen replied, trying to work through it enough to find words for what she felt. Not all that different than therapy. "I'm overwhelmed. I never expected to feel that way again, even with Ethan. I thought I'd moved on from losing Henry. I mean, I still think I did. It's not that I'm still… I'll always love Henry. But he isn't here. So, I said my goodbyes and thought I was ready to move on. It's been three years."

"You lost him so young. I'm sure that's harder."

"Maybe. It's more I thought I'd said all my goodbyes to Henry. We buried him, moved out of that house. What was left? But kissing another man was one thing I didn't expect to be a goodbye to him. I'd only ever kissed Henry before."

"That's not true. You kissed Ben Hutchins to make Henry jealous that one time."

It got a good laugh out of Pen, as she'd forgotten that. "I was *sixteen*."

"Yeah, but it counts."

"Okay, fine. Still. I didn't expect it to be so…" She struggled to find the words. Any words. She'd had this idea of what moving on would feel like. Cathartic. Good. Exciting.

But this wasn't any of those things. Well, it was a little exciting, but fear had been bigger. The unexpected potency, breadth and effect of Ethan's kiss was so much bigger than she'd fully allowed herself to believe was possible.

"Ethan's always been safe. That kiss wasn't safe. That kiss was…" Too big. Too right. A kiss that would change everything when she'd only wanted a little change. Only wanted to feel like a woman instead of a harried mother just trying to get through the day.

She cared about Ethan, she was attracted to Ethan, but that kiss was bigger than those words. It was soul-altering.

"Well, that I understand." Sadie smiled a little dreamily and Pen had no doubt she was remembering her first kiss with Colt. Sadie and Colt had had their share of complications, but Sadie didn't have kids or a dead husband.

"I just thought it'd be nice. To move on. I thought I wanted to feel that again. I do want to feel that again. But…but it's a hell of a lot more complicated a feeling than I thought it'd be."

"Nice." Sadie chuckled a little. "Pen. I know you've done it once before, but there is nothing nice about falling in love."

"There was with Henry!"

"Oh, please. You two broke up like every other week in high school. It was constant drama."

"We were teenagers," Pen grumbled.

"Yeah. Without a lot of baggage—so you created as much as you could, because that's what teenagers do. Now you're thirty. You've got three kids, a late husband, and all *kinds* of baggage. And that's just you. Add Ethan in? Pen, that's *hard*. It's going to be hard and complicated."

"I don't want another hard thing." Which wasn't totally true. She'd just been talking to Ethan about life not being easy and nothing worth it being easy but this... Well, it wasn't fair.

Maybe in losing Henry she'd forgotten about all the hard parts of their relationship, of marriage. Or not forgotten exactly but not given those memories any space because she'd just wanted to remember the good. Nothing wrong with focusing on the good she'd had with him, but there was more to a real, living relationship than good.

Relationships were hard, no matter what. She'd been stupid to think she could waltz around with Ethan having something simple. Stupid to think Ethan would be easy, when he only kept getting harder and more complicated.

"I guess I thought anything I'd have after Henry would be a shadow. Dimmer than that because I loved him so much. But this is just as bright, and so much scarier because I have so much more to lose, and three little girls who could get hurt in all of this. They don't need any more hurt."

Sadie placed a hand over Pen's. "Ethan would never hurt your girls."

"I would have said Colt would never hurt you, but there was a time that's exactly what he did."

Sadie made a face. "Okay, true. And Ethan strikes me as the still waters hiding deep secrets type, which means… You're in for it."

"Gee, thanks."

"He's also one of the best men I know."

"Yeah, there is that. The thing is, it's not that I want to take it back. It's not that it was wrong. It just knocked me off my feet. I wasn't prepared for that. I have to recalibrate to thinking this might be something…bigger." She let her head fall into her hands. "And after all that poking at him to kiss me, I ran away."

Sadie made a small sound and when Pen looked up she glared at her little sister.

"I'm sorry. It's just…" She made another choked sound as if trying to swallow down laughter.

"It isn't *funny*, Sadie."

"It kind of is." Sadie attempted to keep her expression serious. "Or it will be. Some day. In the future."

"I feel like I have to know what I want. Exactly. Or I risk…everything. My friendship with Ethan. Hurting my girls."

"Hurting yourself."

Life is hurt, babe. Henry used to say that a lot and it had always irritated her, but she'd never told him because he had to see awful things at work. She knew he had to believe it. And she'd worked hard to have a place for him to come home to and see that life was also beautiful.

"I think it's an impossible task to know exactly what you want, Pen, because that'll change. Life changes. So, maybe you simplify that a little bit."

"Simplify?"

"Instead of trying to plan out exactly what you want, maybe just decide what you're willing to work for. And what you're not. Do you want to fight for something with Ethan? Because it's going to be a fight and it's going to be complicated. Or do you want to protect your heart and the girls' hearts?"

"You can't protect your heart, Sadie. Not really."

"Well, then, isn't that your answer?"

It was hers, but she knew it wasn't Ethan's. Her reaction might not have made sense to him, but it wasn't like that kiss had changed anything he thought. Sure, he'd initiated it, but then he'd said they shouldn't have.

"I wasn't ready," Pen murmured. "If I'd been ready maybe I could have handled it better. Smarter."

"I don't think we're ever *ready*. I wasn't."

"You dove in headfirst with Colt."

Sadie grinned. "Yeah, but it doesn't mean I was ready for it."

Pen turned to her sister, for the first time in her life realizing Sadie had a better grasp on what she was doing and what she was going through than anyone. Sadie had done this. Maybe she hadn't had a dead husband and kids as baggage, but she'd built something with one of the men her parents had brought home to care for as their own.

Pen had never relied on Sadie for advice before, but Sadie was the only one she could now. "How do you navigate all of it?"

Sadie blinked. "Are you asking me for advice?"

"Don't act like that's never happened before."

"It has literally *never* happened before."

"Sadie."

"Okay. I'm no good at advice. I don't know how we made it work. Colt had to accept some things about himself. I had to learn how to be better at expressing my feelings. But most of all we both had to get to a place where we were willing to be honest, to be uncomfortable, to let down some things we'd been carrying that didn't serve us. I couldn't *make* that happen. We both had to make that decision individually, and a lot of crap stuff had to happen to get Colt to a place where he could let some of his stuff go. I believe you dropping an f-bomb at him is one of those things."

Pen managed a laugh. "Oh, I was so mad at him. He was being such an idiot."

"He was. Ethan will be too."

"You're really bad at the cheering-up thing."

"Oh, I thought I was giving advice. That's *never* cheering."

Pen laughed. "I guess I just have to wrap my head around this being bigger than I expected."

Sadie slid an arm around Pen's shoulders. "I think you're an expert at that, Pen. And Ethan doesn't stand a chance. You know, eventually."

"He's going to make me work for it."

"He's going to make you *struggle* for it," Sadie said, giving her a squeeze. "It'll be worth it. At least, it was for me."

Pen sighed. She'd worked and struggled for love once. Would it really be worth doing it a second time? Would it put a burden on her girls she should avoid until they were grown?

She supposed she'd have to figure that out too.

Chapter Eleven

P EN AVOIDED HIM. Ethan wanted to be relieved at every day that passed where he wasn't in a room alone with her. Where she didn't demand they talk about that kiss.

But nothing that happened made any sense to him. She'd initiated all that. Poked and poked until he'd been stupid enough to forget himself.

Then she'd run away and avoided him as Christmas barreled down on them.

Had she felt nothing? It had rocked him off his axis and she'd been repulsed by it after all her pushing.

He wanted to believe that, but it didn't work. If she hadn't felt anything, she would have told him. Just like she'd said to him—he would have let her down gently if he wasn't interested, and she would have let him down gently if that kiss had been nothing to her.

It was who they were.

But even knowing what she would have done, he couldn't figure out what she was doing.

And are too much of a coward to ask.

He went to work. He went back to the Martin house. He helped with Christmas prep—often picking up things at various stores that Pen texted him. Not that she ever asked him to do anything in person. She always waited until he was at work and sent him a text.

He let her avoid, and did a lot of avoiding himself. He convinced himself it was the answer no matter how he felt heavier each day. It was just Christmas was all.

The Christmas season was never the best of times at work. The stress and loneliness of the season often brought out the worst in people already barely holding on. It weighed on Ethan every year, reminding him of things he'd promised himself he'd forgotten or let go.

He found himself going back to his apartment after work, changing into normal clothes and then just…being alone.

It was a bad habit. A spiral he knew better than to indulge in, but that kiss with Pen and all the Christmas cheer that choked him everywhere he went fought against that reasonable knowledge.

Tonight was worse. Christmas was just days away, and he'd never been a fan of Christmas. He usually went and visited his sister's grave after work. Then went home and wished for New Year's Day when this would all end. Usually, he got through it because he could. Because he refused not to.

But this year a phone call from a friend he'd made at the prison his father was at made everything worse. The heads-up on what was likely coming.

Dad was getting out next month. Good behavior. After

what he'd done.

Sometimes Ethan wondered why he'd dedicated his life to upholding the law, when lawyers and judges and a corrupt system undermined it half the time.

The knock at the door made him sigh. This gray fog around him wasn't healthy; he knew that. But he could handle it. Once the calendar changed over to a new year everything would be fine and back to normal.

Except Dad would be out.

He stared at the door wishing he could ignore it. Maybe it was just Colt worried about him. He hadn't even told Colt he'd kissed Pen. Of course, Pen had probably told Sadie, which meant Colt knew. Unless Pen had kept it to herself too.

God, he hoped so. Hoped everyone kept it to themselves and forgot about it.

It could be Bracken, home a day early wanting to crash here instead of out at the farm, but he would have called.

When Ethan opened the door to Pen, he had to resist the urge to slam it in her face.

"I know I'm the last person you want to see," she said in that maddeningly calm, pleasant way she'd been talking to him lately.

"Not the last," Ethan muttered as she slid past him and into his apartment.

Pen wrinkled her nose as she slid off her jacket and laid it over the back of his kitchen chair. "This is stark."

"I've been living at the farm."

"I doubt that's why it's stark." She turned to face him, clutching her purse in one hand. Her expression was placid and her voice was mild, but the death grip on her purse gave her away.

It didn't seem she wanted to be here any more than he wanted her here.

Or how badly you want her here.

"Dad was worried about you, and I was at the hospital. They gave me a shorter cast and cleared me to drive." She waved her arm in the air awkwardly. "So, I said I'd stop by on my way home. It looks like he was right to be worried. What are you doing? Didn't you get off two hours ago?"

"It's not the day, Pen. I just need to be alone. I'll be out to the farm in a bit." He pointed at the still-open door and when she crossed to him, he thought she meant to leave. She was actually going to listen and leave him be.

What had he done that she would do *that*?

He almost reached out to stop her. Beg her to stay, to talk things through.

But he'd never been a man who put his own needs before what had to be done. The call he'd received felt like a karmic reminder. Any fantasies he'd had about actually making something work had to die now.

Which meant she should go. If they avoided each other enough, this would all fade away. No hurt feelings. Nothing too complicated. A blip to be forgotten.

But Pen didn't leave. She removed his hand from the door and closed it herself. With her still inside.

"The last thing you need is to be alone. Clearly." She reached out and cupped his cheek, concern in her eyes as her thumb moved back and forth.

Ethan felt like she'd shattered all that strength inside of him. If he kept looking at her, he'd fall apart on the outside too. So, he turned away from her hand and her concern.

But all he could seem to do was press his palms against the wall, leaning against it with his eyes screwed shut, trying to fight it back into place. If he could get her to leave, everything would be okay. He'd put it all back into place. He just needed her to leave.

She didn't, of course. Instead she pressed her hand to his back.

He wouldn't break, wouldn't allow himself to. But he'd never been so close to it. Not around Pen, or anyone. Except her mother.

Pen had never been Susannah. She didn't take care of him. She hadn't saved him.

But she leaned her cheek against his back, wrapped her good arm around him, and for a second he thought she would. He *wanted* her to fix this awfulness inside of him.

But no one could. He had to believe no one could, even while she touched him gently. Hugged him in comfort and care.

He wouldn't survive it. It would break him. He'd go back to being…whatever he'd been before. Out of control and desperate. He'd built his life separate from the child he'd been. He couldn't go back there.

She had to leave. Which meant the only way to survive, to get her away, was to be the opposite of what she was to him. No gentleness. No care.

He pushed off the wall, turning around to face her. She stepped back, startled, but he only grabbed her and pulled her back to him.

Then he kissed her. Not like he had a few weeks ago. No, he gave himself leave to kiss her any which way he pleased. Rough, greedy. Desperate. He poured too much into that kiss and he refused to care. It was wrong, but it would scare her into leaving. Into running away again.

Or you just desperately need her.

He pushed that voice away, even though it kept trying to win. Because she didn't just *take* the kiss, she kissed him back. As if she had her own hurts and grief. Her good arm grasped his shoulder and she poured herself into him as if they were the only two people in the world.

For a few moments, he wanted to believe they were. So, he touched her. Instead of holding her, he slid his hands under her shirt. Moved his hands over the smooth skin of her abdomen, her back.

She sighed against his mouth. Like this was right and good instead of a mistake he couldn't seem to stop himself from making.

"You don't want this." She couldn't. He couldn't help himself, but she could. Had to. "You can't."

"Yes, I do," she replied, breathless and pulling at his T-shirt.

"Pen."

"I do want this. I want you. And you want me." She kissed him, devastated him inside and out. He tried to move away, but she held him in place.

"It can just be tonight," she whispered. "That's okay. Just tonight. Just us. I want you, Ethan. Even if it's only once."

He knew it for the lie it was, but he was too... He hated the word, but he felt fragile. And with every touch she swept that away until he felt alive again. Strong again.

I want you.

No one wanted him. No one asked him for more than he could give. He wouldn't let them. Except Pen. Always Pen.

She tugged at his shirt again, and this time he pulled it off. She let out a shaky breath, placing her hand on his chest, splaying out her fingers.

Stop this. It was an echo in his mind, but no matter how much his brain seemed tethered to the real world, his body was here. With her. In this fantasy one.

He pulled off her shirt, making sure it didn't tangle with her cast. She wasn't wearing a bra and he could only stare like some kind of moronic pre-teen who didn't know what to do when faced with breasts.

"Bras are a little hard with a cast."

"I don't mind."

She laughed, and her smile was just for him. What was he doing?

"We shouldn't do this."

She stepped forward, wrapping both arms around him. She was warm and soft and she pressed herself against him, watching him the whole time with humor still curving her mouth. "Oh, Ethan. It's too late for that."

It was another lie. *Just tonight. Too late.* Of course it wasn't, on either score, but she was so sure and that was the last thing he was tonight.

So, he kissed her anyway. Touched her. Told her she was beautiful and let himself go. He kissed her into his room, caressed her into his bed, and forgot who and what he was when he entered her on a groan they shared.

The more he touched, tasted, the more she moved against him, the more whole he felt. Stitched together. Cured of all that jangled inside of him because there was only her and this.

She cried out her release with his name on her lips, and he followed. Everything that joining together with her had solved inside of him broke apart as they fell apart. She'd hollowed him out and taken away every battlement he'd built in years and years of building.

She curled up into him. Solace and strength and…

Very much not yours.

She had too many other people. Too much else. She thought she understood him, but it was only because he kept it all to himself.

Couldn't you keep doing that?

He got off the bed and disappeared into the bathroom to take care of practicalities. When he returned, he didn't let himself get sucked back in. It would be a bigger catastrophe than the one he'd already made.

He stood in the bathroom doorway, lead all the way

through no matter how hard his heart beat against it.

She looked beautiful in his bed. Sleepy and rumpled and everything he'd ever wanted. And known he'd never ever have. Not even this. Something fleeting and wrong.

So wrong.

"You have to go," he said gruffly.

She sat up in his bed, holding the sheet to her breast. She didn't look startled or surprised or even hurt. She looked...resigned. "You're going to tell me this was a mistake."

"It *was* a mistake." He didn't have the wherewithal to tell her all the things he needed to. He didn't have anything left. "I just need you to go."

She began to gather her clothes and put them back on. The shorter cast had definitely made her a lot more mobile. But he found himself...surprised she wasn't arguing.

"All right," she said once she was dressed. The cool, regal way she said that felt like the nail in the coffin. It was over. His life with the Martins was perfectly and utterly destroyed. His own weaknesses failing him yet again.

She walked toward him, not the door. There wasn't resignation in her eyes anymore. No, there was something closer to fire. But when she spoke it was so *calm*. Like she'd planned this all out. Like she knew exactly what steps she was taking.

Only every step she took dismantled some piece of his life.

"I'll give you tonight, Ethan, because you're used to dealing alone," she said solemnly, standing in front of him. Her eyes alight with something. "But you won't be anymore."

Alone was what he was. What he *had* to be. "Pen—"

"That was amazing," she said, pointing at the bed. "*That* was right. You might not want to believe it, but you know it."

He meant to shake his head, to argue with her, but all he could seem to do was stand rooted to the spot.

"That first kiss scared me, I'll admit it. Not for probably any of the reasons you made up in your head, not that you bothered asking. But I didn't offer to tell you either because I needed some time to…reconcile myself to some things. Because that kiss was so much bigger than I was prepared for."

She kept moving toward him, this force he had to resist somehow.

"But I'm not scared anymore. I refuse to be. I've lost too much in my life to keep being scared. So, you're not going to like this, but I love you."

He had to look away, to turn away. He had no problem resisting that because it was the last thing he wanted, the last thing she needed. "Don't say that to me."

"Too late. Take your night to wallow. To convince yourself all your baggage is holding you back. We'll talk tomorrow. And God help you if you try to make a run for it like Colt did."

"I don't want—"

But she was dressed and out the bedroom door, and then the front door, slamming it behind her.

Chapter Twelve

PEN WASN'T SURE what she felt. She thought maybe if there were goddesses or superheroes, this is what they'd feel like. Powerful. *Right.* And a little disappointed that mere mortals didn't know what they were doing.

She sighed as she pulled up in front of the house. She wasn't even mad anymore, or frustrated. She just felt badly for Ethan.

For so long he'd hidden that wounded heart under such a perfect layer of stoicism and decency no one had noticed. Not really. But no matter what she'd begun to suspect and find in him the past few weeks, tonight had shown her the full picture.

Ethan needed love. And he needed to let some things go, and acknowledge some other things. She'd told him she'd give him tonight because he was used to being alone, but the truth was she didn't know how to reach him.

She got out of the car. The stars twinkled above like diamonds, and the air was cold. The Christmas lights shone brightly, and in the distance she could see the same colored lights on Sadie and Colt's cabin.

And she belonged here. No matter what happened with

Ethan, she belonged exactly here. That would give her the strength to do whatever it took to get through to that very stubborn man.

She walked inside then stopped short at the sight of her baby sister at the table with Sadie. "Mack. You're home early."

"Weather was going to be bad tomorrow so we headed out this morning." Mack raised an eyebrow. "You look rumpled."

"Oh my *God*," Sadie breathed, taking in her appearance.

"What?" Mack demanded. "Pen have a boyfriend no one told me about?"

But Sadie didn't look at Mack. She kept her wide-eyed gaze on Pen. "Dad told you to check in on Ethan on your way home."

"Oh my *God*," Mack echoed. "What on earth have I missed? First you." She pointed at Sadie with some disgust. "Now you."

Sadie turned to Mack, all wide-eyed innocence. "Who does that leave you?"

Mack scowled at Sadie and lifted her middle finger.

Sadie grinned up at Pen and it was then Pen noticed the bottle of wine between her sisters. Yes, that was exactly what she needed. She grabbed the wine bottle off the table and took a long gulp straight from the bottle.

"So, what's the story?" Mack asked. The glass of wine in front of her was mostly full, but Sadie's was empty.

Pen took another very unladylike swig, wishing she had

her father's whiskey instead. "It's not a very good one. Not yet."

"Oh, Pen, I do love your battle light when it's not aimed at me." Mack grinned.

"Sit down. Spill," Sadie said, patting the chair next to her.

"Where are the girls?"

"They're having a wrapping party over at my cabin with Dad and Colt. In other words, the men are conning your girls into wrapping the presents they bought for us."

"All right." Pen took a seat. Mack offered her glass, but Pen shook her head. "I slept with Ethan."

"I can't believe you two," Mack muttered disgustedly.

"I didn't actually plan to. When Dad asked me to stop by, I didn't want to. I still hadn't figured anything out. He kissed me a few weeks ago and it was a lot...*more* than I expected," Pen explained to Mac since Sadie already knew that part. "But he opened the door and I immediately knew I'd been an idiot. You can't figure things out like that. All on your own, forever turning over the same problem. You need to acknowledge it and face it—especially with the person you're trying to work things out with."

"*You* do. Not everyone does."

Pen looked pointedly at her youngest sister. "Everyone, Sis. Everyone. But he was... Something happened. Beyond me. I don't know what, but he had more on his shoulders than he usually does." And he hadn't told her. Hadn't even tried to. He'd tried to scare her away.

"I… I knew he would do this. I knew it would end with him thinking it was a mistake." There'd been no surprise there. The surprise had been wanting to make love with him anyway—even knowing he'd regret it. She couldn't explain that to herself. She'd wanted him on the basic level of wanting someone, but she'd also wanted to prove he couldn't scare her away. She wouldn't let him. "I knew he'd think it was a mistake going in, but…it was still amazing."

"Because you love him," Mack said, and though she clearly wasn't pleased the disgust in her tone was muted.

"No. Because he loves you," Sadie corrected. "I don't know much, but I think loving someone and not having them love you back wouldn't be amazing. It was amazing because you know he loves you."

"I think he does," Pen agreed, trying to breathe through that. Love was so much more than she'd bargained for, so much bigger and quicker. But just as she'd told him earlier, they were right together. Maybe right didn't always come with good timing. And maybe that was okay.

"He needed me tonight. He *needs* us. I've always loved Ethan one way or another, but it took this whole month to understand him."

Sadie twisted her engagement ring around on her finger. "Do you think you can get through to him?"

"I don't know. Maybe I can't." Pen sucked in a deep breath. That knowledge scared her most of all. "But I have to try." She thought of the love she'd had and lost—both her mother's and her husband's. Loss hurt. So much. But love…

"Life's too precious not to try. He looked so… He was alone in that apartment and he just looked gray."

"Christmas is always a hard time for him," Sadie noted.

"It shouldn't be. He has all of us."

"Sometimes having people doesn't help with…things," Mack said, staring hard at her glass.

Pen frowned at that, but she could only deal with one hardheaded, emotionally distant person at a time. "I guess it doesn't. Especially when you won't even admit what's wrong." She gave Mack a pointed look, but didn't press it. "I mean, that was my problem. I was trying to push down all of the feelings I didn't want to deal with. I channeled all that anxiety into something else. But it comes out anyway. One way or another."

"Ethan doesn't strike me as anxious," Sadie replied with a thoughtful frown. "He doesn't strike me as anything that…frenetic."

"No, he's not frenetic. He's not even out of control—though that's probably how he considered what he did tonight. He holds himself separate."

"Some of us are just more naturally introverted," Mack pointed out.

"Yes, that's true, and that's certainly part of it. But he takes great pains to give the illusion of someone who's always there. He's the first to offer to help. No one ever doubts Ethan will step in and do the right thing."

"But?" Sadie prompted.

"He distances himself. Yes, he'll pick up milk. He watches the girls if there's an emergency. He'd drive me home from Christkindlmarkt even though it's the last thing he wants to do. He's *here* when it's important, but he's holding himself back. In the periphery. He doesn't get in the thick of things and argue. He doesn't wade into fraught discussions. He acts, but he doesn't join." She thought about what he'd told her about Colt and Bracken threatening Henry before they got married. He'd held himself separate even from that—because it would have required being involved. Being connected.

"Why would someone keep themselves separate like that?" Sadie asked. "When he has to know we all love him."

Both Pen and Sadie's gaze lifted to Mack.

"Don't you both look at me. This is about Ethan."

"But you do it. You keep yourself far away," Pen said gently. "You could tell us why, you know."

Mack stared at the table for a long time, so long Pen really thought she wouldn't say anything. Until she did.

"Being here is complicated. The rodeo isn't." She looked directly at Pen, not at Sadie. "I don't want to get into this right now, okay?"

Pen didn't know what exactly about being home would be complicated for Mack, but it wasn't like Mack to be honest. Usually she'd try to piss everyone off until they left her alone. So, Pen decided to give her some space, since she'd asked for it instead of acting out.

"Okay."

Mack shrugged. "If Ethan distances himself, it's because

something about joining the fray hurts."

"Hurts. Or he's scared of it hurting," Pen mused. "He's avoiding complicated. He's avoiding feeling deeply and..." It hit her then. Not quite like a lightning bolt—more like a succession of blows.

The things he'd said to her since Thanksgiving. The way he'd acted tonight afterward.

Her staying and talking would have been complicated. Pieces of it would have hurt him. So, what had he done?

"Tomorrow morning when Ethan comes by, assuming he actually does, can you guys keep the girls and Dad occupied?"

"Of course," Sadie replied. "Consider it done."

ETHAN DIDN'T WANT to face Pen, but ignoring this wouldn't make it go away. Besides, he'd slipped up and made a mistake, which meant he had to face the consequences.

And make sure he made it clear there could be no more. He'd tell her everything and then she'd understand. No matter how many times he told himself that, he wasn't altogether sure it was true.

He'd make it true. He had to. He got out of his car and faced the house. He'd go in there, say his piece, and leave. Come New Year's, they'd forget this aberration of a month had ever happened.

They had to.

But before he stepped toward the house he heard some kind of commotion coming from the goat barn. The voices were high-pitched and Ethan peeked his head in the door.

Addie and Brynn were facing off, little hands curled into fists. They were yelling at each other, which Ethan figured was usual enough. He'd seen the Martin sisters do just the same well into adulthood.

But then Brynn lunged at Addie, knocking her down. The two wrestled on the ground as goats bleated around them, almost completely muffled by the girls yelling.

Ethan waded through the herd of goats. Much as he would have left the girls to their yelling, he couldn't leave them to hurt one another.

Since Brynn was on top, he grabbed her. She didn't stop swinging her fists and kicking her legs as he hefted her off Addie who scrambled to her feet.

Addie stood there looking smug while Brynn kept trying to get to her. Ethan was a little surprised at how strong she was—he almost lost a hold of her twice.

"That's enough," he finally ordered in a commanding voice that had Brynn freezing and Addie blinking in surprise. "What on earth has gotten into you two?"

"I hate her! I hate her! She's mean and stupid and I *hate* her." Brynn kicked again, but tears leaked from the corners of her eyes even as she furiously blinked them back.

"What are you two doing in here alone?"

"Daisy got a splinter, so Sadie took her over to her cabin," Addie replied, lifting her chin haughtily. "Before that, Colt asked Mack for help with one of his horses and Grandpa went into town to get donuts. *I said* we could handle things in here by ourselves, but then Brynn acted like a big baby."

"You're mean and rude and I *hate* you," Brynn screamed.

"So you two decided to have a brawl on Christmas Eve?"

"*I* didn't," Addie replied, making a face at Brynn who started wiggling and trying to get out of his grasp again.

He looked at Addie, who had her arms folded across her chest and looked like her mom if not in coloring or face, in disapproving stance. Brynn was still wriggling in his grasp, angry and desperate to inflict harm.

"Is anyone hurt?" Both girls shook their heads. It wasn't his place to stick his nose in their sibling fight, but at the same time it was Christmas Eve and he'd already caused Pen enough grief. "Brynn. You head on over to Sadie and Colt's cabin. You can yell and stomp the whole way there, but taking your anger out on your sister is wrong."

She blinked even more rapidly, sucking in a breath. Her eyes were wide and she was studying him, as if deciding whether he had any right to tell her what to do.

None at all.

But she nodded, her little chin wobbling even as she tried to firm her mouth. Ethan put her on her feet and she dramatically flung her head away from Addie as she left the barn.

Ethan knew he should leave it at that, but he couldn't

seem to make himself do what he knew he should. *Quite the theme with the Martin-Wakefield women, isn't it?*

"What was that about?"

Addie lifted her chin again, looking so haughty Ethan might have found it amusing in a different situation. "She thinks if she's good enough, Santa will bring Mom a new husband. She's stupid. And too old to think stupid things. So I told her the truth."

Something *very* uncomfortable hitched in his gut, but that had to do with him not Addie. "What truth?"

"There's no such thing as Santa. And she got all mad about it and acted like a big, stupid baby."

"It isn't right to hurt her feelings like that. She's your sister."

"What do you know? You don't have a sister. You don't have anyone."

"I did." He hadn't meant to say that. But *anyone* had hit hard enough that the words tumbled out. He felt even worse about it when Addie looked up at him like she'd been slapped.

"She died?" Addie asked, because this girl was very well acquainted with senseless, early death and what past tense meant.

"Yeah."

"I'm sorry."

"Me, too."

"Doesn't mean Brynn isn't a stupid baby," Addie muttered under her breath.

Ethan wanted to smile but he pressed his lips together to keep his expression serious. "Would it have hurt to let her believe that?"

"Yes! She'd wake up on Christmas morning and be stupidly sad that *Santa* didn't magically put some guy under our tree that Mom would somehow marry. I'm saving her a lot of trouble, and Mom the trouble of having to make her feel better. I did the right thing."

It was hard to argue with that logic, because it *was* logic, and in her own way Addie was trying to protect the people she loved.

But all Ethan could think about was what Pen had said back when she'd broken her arm. That Brynn wanted to act like she didn't believe, but she had too much imagination not to believe in magic.

"I understand that." But there was something about Addie's smugness that reminded him of the Martin girls and their sisterly fights. "But I want you to think about if you really did it to spare her, or if you did it because you were mad and wanted to hurt her feelings. The first one is dangerous, because sometimes hope and belief are good things...even if there's no real foundation for them. The second one is flat-out wrong, and I think you're better than that."

Her eyebrows drew together, and she looked at him like he'd kicked one of the goats right in front of her. Not just hurt, but a little horrified.

She didn't say anything. She turned on a heel and

marched out of the barn.

Smooth. Real smooth.

He followed her, and no matter how she stormed his long strides caught up with her as she flung herself into the house. He stepped into the kitchen where Pen sat at the table, looking serene, but she frowned when Addie stomped in beside him.

"I thought you were—"

"I'm going back to bed," Addie announced, continuing her stomping all the way upstairs.

Pen's confused gaze lifted to Ethan. "What happened?"

Faced with her in this kitchen, he didn't have the words to explain all of that. "I caught her and Brynn fighting in the goat barn."

Pen's frowned deepened. "About what?"

He really couldn't get into *that*. "I'm not sure. But Brynn's with Mack and Sadie and Daisy. I thought maybe it was better if Addie had some time to cool off."

Pen nodded. "That's probably best. Brynn has a bit of a temper."

"I noticed."

"I don't know where she gets it from. We Martins are such a calm, even-tempered people." She said it seriously, so seriously he had to, once again, fight the urge to smile. She let out a sigh, giving a glimpse to the staircase Addie had stormed up, then looked back to the table. "I'll have to give her a bit of time to cool off too or she won't tell me anything."

Then she turned her gaze to him. She fixed him with that calm *I know everything* look. "Sit. We have a lot to talk about."

Chapter Thirteen

P EN HAD SPENT most of the night going over what she wanted to say, how she wanted to say it. Addie's tantrum had fractured her focus though—half of her brain was mulling over what the two girls could have had such a heated argument over on Christmas Eve.

Which unsurprisingly was what Ethan was focused on.

"I shouldn't have interfered."

"Why not?"

"I... I'm not their parent."

"No, but last time I checked this was family by committee. You're a part of that."

"I—"

"Whether you want to be or not. You've braided Brynn's hair. Watched all three girls when I went to visit Dad in the hospital. You've been buying birthday presents for them since they were born. You, Colt, and Bracken—you're all a part of the conglomeration of adults that has raised them and loved them through good and bad. So. Step in. Be there. Offer advice. If I don't like it, you'll be sure to know."

She could tell he wanted to argue, but he nodded instead. How many times in their lives had he done that?

Swallowed down his arguments and objections? Because it was easier to go along. Not like some kind of pushover. No. Ethan gave the illusion of doing what other people wanted.

In the end, he usually did what he wanted anyway.

She admired that about him. It kept the peace, and avoided a lot of pointless arguing.

But sometimes peace wasn't the answer.

"Did you have anything else to say before I tell you how wrong you were about last night?" she asked, doing her best to sound regal and sure even while her heart thundered in her chest with nerves and fear she'd say all the wrong things.

But she was Susannah Martin's daughter. She'd find a way to get through to this man, just like her mother had when Ethan was a boy.

"My father is getting out of jail next month."

Pen opened her mouth to say something, but since she hadn't even considered he would come up with *that*, she could only shut it. That must have been what was weighing on him last night.

Very carefully he linked his fingers together in front of him on the table, and he stared at those links. Once upon a time she'd mistaken that for calm, but it wasn't. Just like her he held himself the most still when the storm raged within.

He had to let the storm out.

"I'm sorry, Ethan," she offered, and it was genuine. She might not have been around, or know the details, but she knew what his father had done hurt Ethan. Shamed him, even if he had no real connection to Abe Thompson beyond biology.

She couldn't pretend she knew what it was like to suffer through parents like Ethan had, but she failed to imagine why he was bringing this up *now*, especially when he was usually so private about his family.

"I don't need your sympathy. I need you to understand."

But she didn't. At all.

"I know you think last night was right, and maybe if nothing else existed in the world it would have been, but things exist. People exist."

"Is this supposed to be news to me?"

He sighed, some of that composure slipping. "I have to tell you what happened between Susannah and my father and then maybe you can understand."

"All right."

"No one knows this story. Fritz might, but he's never given me any indication he did."

"And you've never asked him."

Another piece of his iron composure moved. "Well, no, but…" He shook his head, his fingers linked so hard together his knuckles were white. "It doesn't matter."

Pen figured it proved her point, but she'd let him have his piece before she made it.

"I have a sister—I had a sister. She passed away around the same time your mother did."

Pen blinked. She'd known he had secrets, but to have such a big piece of his life be such a surprise rocked her.

"She was four years older than me, and when I was ten,

my father had her involuntarily committed. He said she was…all sorts of things that weren't true. Even at ten I knew they weren't true. But he's a convincing man who knows how to manipulate people, and my mother always supported him. Amy didn't want to follow his rules, she wanted to *escape* him, but she wasn't a danger to herself or anyone else. Not until he put her in a *facility*."

He spoke so calmly, clearly a practiced speech. But he couldn't practice the anguish out of his eyes.

"When she turned eighteen, she got out, but then she seemed hell-bent on proving everything he'd said about her. She died of a drug overdose."

"I'm sorry, Ethan." Pen reached out and put her hand over his linked ones. "I had no idea."

"My father broke her. He really did. And I was young, but I could see what he was doing even before he had her committed—when he started talking about it that's when I started… I didn't want to end up some place I didn't choose. So that's when I started stealing, fighting, trying to get in real trouble that would take me away before he could send me away. Instead, Susannah found me. And she promised to keep me safe."

"She kept that promise."

"She did. But she had to lie to do it."

Pen withdrew her hand, couldn't help the way surprise made her want to run away. She *wouldn't*, but she was starting to worry this was going to be even harder than she'd thought—and she'd known she had a battle in front of her.

"She couldn't get concrete evidence to hurt my father no matter how hard she tried, and she tried. She didn't want me to know, but her and Fritz were starting to fight about it. How much time she was spending on this extracurricular project. How much time it was taking away from you girls."

"Ethan, they were always fighting about her job, and they always made up. Because no matter how much Dad struggled with the way she dedicated her life to her job, he understood it was...part of her. Important to her."

"Well, regardless, she felt like she had to keep that promise to me. So, she went to my father and told him she had evidence she didn't have, and that she wouldn't arrest him if he left town, and left me behind. She knew enough about the women he'd harassed to make it seem like she had concrete proof, but she didn't."

"And he left?"

"Not without threatening revenge."

"He never got that revenge."

"Only because she died, Pen. I need you to understand that. After she died, my father contacted me and said how lucky it was Susannah had died, because he'd finally found what he'd needed to get her removed from her job."

"He was lying. Mom never did anything that would have jeopardized her job."

"He wasn't lying. She lied to him to save me—that's jeopardizing."

It was such a strange thing. Sadie saying Mom swore when Pen didn't remember her mother being less than perfect had been confronting in the moment, but this was... Mom had lied. It was completely incongruous with the mother she remembered, the *lectures* she remembered.

She believed Ethan though. Mom had lied, but for a reason. For this man. Because she'd wanted to save him. No matter what Pen remembered as a child or young teenager, she could understand that truth wouldn't have mattered to her mother if someone needed saving.

"How do you know your father wasn't lying about the revenge?" Pen asked gently. "From the way it sounds to me he's an expert liar, and saying something like that to you was the perfect manipulation."

Ethan opened his mouth, but instead of words coming out he only shut it, forehead wrinkling in confusion. "It doesn't matter," he finally said, as if he could say it fiercely enough to make it true. "The point is, my father doesn't forgive and forget no matter how often I've heard him preach it. He believes in retribution—and I'm an integral reason why he's in jail. The girl he assaulted—her parents had been intimidated into not supporting her. Into encouraging her not to press charges. He'd gotten to them, but he couldn't get to me."

"So, you think when he gets out he's going to try and enact some kind of revenge?"

"I'm certain of it."

She might be better at understanding Ethan underneath the stoicism, but she couldn't work her way through this. "What... What does that have to do with last night?"

"Anyone I'm close to is in the line of fire."

"So?"

"So. So, I won't put you or your girls in that line of fire."

She tried to ignore the irritation simmering inside of her. This was what he genuinely felt. Even if it was stupid and wrong. "But you're here," she said, pointing at the table though she meant bigger than his physical *here*. "You're part of our family. If he's going to hurt you, he's going to hurt us."

He looked at her like she'd spoken some foreign language, and as hard as Pen had known this was going to be, understanding these boys and their simple refusal to believe in love when they'd been offered so much of it baffled her.

But she'd been loved from the very beginning. There'd never been a question if her parents were supportive or cared. She'd always known.

So, the fight she had ahead of her wasn't against the man he was. No, it was against the scared, lonely, unloved boy he'd been.

She had to start where Mom had left off.

"NO, I—" ETHAN shook his head against Pen's arguments. They seemed so rational, but that was just emotion talking. It wasn't reality. "You don't understand."

"You think you're doing this noble thing to keep me separate, to protect my girls, but that doesn't make any sense."

She grabbed his hands as if she knew he was five seconds from bolting. "You're part of us one way or another. You *have* to know that."

Whether he did or not, he ignored that statement. "You don't understand him."

"No, I don't, but neither do you. You're a good man, Ethan. You can't possibly understand why he does the things he does—and you can't possibly predict the things he'll do."

He couldn't argue with that. He didn't understand the man his father was, which made it all that much worse when he saw him in the mirror or heard Abe's voice in his own. But he knew enough. Because of that, he understood better than she ever would. "I know he'll try to hurt me. That I know. Which makes my connection to anyone dangerous. Maybe if it was just you, Pen, that wouldn't be such an impossible thing to fight. But you have those three little girls, and I can't... I can't handle bringing them into this. Not this."

"You've really convinced yourself that this is the reason you're balking at an *us*," she said, folding her arms across her chest just as Addie had done in the barn, but he couldn't find any humor in those connections because she didn't believe him.

Why that shook his foundations didn't make any sense to him. She didn't have to believe him. "It *is* the reason," he said making sure to enunciate, to hold her gaze. To prove it to her.

To yourself.

"No. No, I don't think so. It doesn't make sense. Maybe it makes sense in your head—but we all love you, would do anything to protect you. Me, Colt. My father. All of us. Whether you love me or not, him coming after you doesn't change what we'd do. Years ago or today—you're a part of us."

"You don't understand."

"You keep saying that, but I do. I think I understand it better than you do. Because this isn't about protection, Ethan. You would have left us a long time ago if that were true. Cut ties if you ever truly thought you were a danger to us."

"I wouldn't let him ruin my life."

"Bull. What are you doing right now? You've created quite a story, but it doesn't ring true. You're not trying to protect *us*. This is about protecting yourself."

"From what? From you? From the way you've convinced yourself you're in love with me?" The words were harsh, but of course he should know by now she didn't wilt at his harsh.

"No. It isn't about me. I'm the culmination of your issues, but it started a long time ago. It's about you, Ethan. You want to believe you're protecting everyone else, but the truth is you're only protecting yourself from all those big emotions. Keeping yourself just enough separate that things don't have to hurt so badly."

He turned away from her, which he realized was a mistake after his body had already gone through the motions. It was cowardly. He had to look her down. Prove she was wrong. But he couldn't make himself do it.

"It's easy to give half," she said earnestly.

Each word felt like a wound, like an attack. If it hurt this much, it couldn't be right. She couldn't be right.

"Easier than running away. Easier than giving it all. You gave it all to my mother and what happened? She died."

Ethan whirled on her abruptly. "I'm not Colt. Don't put his issues on me."

She stood there looking so calm he wanted to scream and rage and throw things, but her eyes held him in place. Because there was a sadness there.

One you put there.

"Yours aren't all that different. You don't think you're poison like Colt did. I get that. But you think you can save yourself from the hurt. Not because of anything you deserve or not, but because you're afraid. You want to save yourself from it by giving just enough you don't have to hurt."

"I hurt." The words came out on a rasp, as painful as all of what she was saying. As painful as all that had come before.

She moved to him, and even when he pulled away from her hand she reached out to touch his face. To hold it steady so he looked at her while she spoke.

"Of course you do. We all do. Life does. That's why you let love in. But you have to acknowledge what's wrong or it festers, and nothing gets in but fear and pain. I know we're not the same person, but that's where I was last month. Bottling it up and holding it in and telling myself all that panic and pain was something else—because the something else was easier than dealing with all that *grief*."

"What magical hurt do I need to acknowledge, Pen? What thing can I chant to fix everything for me?"

She kept hold of his face, kept her gaze on his as if he hadn't been derisive at all. "Losing Mom. Losing your sister."

"She's gone. They're both gone. That's life." Painful life. One that seemed to bloom around them. But it was what it was. "What is there to acknowledge?"

"That you loved your sister and couldn't protect her. That my mother was the first person you trusted and loved, and she died. Too soon and with too little warning."

"I know all those things," he returned, thinking it would be easier to be stabbed than to deal with this. He so desperately wanted to leave. To separate himself from this, but it would prove her point and if he did that, he'd never…

Keep her and the girls safe from his father. That was all he wanted to do. None of this other…made-up stuff she was pushing at him.

"It was hard for me to lose her, of course, but I was surrounded by love. Always. Day one to this second. Losing her, even losing Henry, those were terrible, painful losses that I'll always grieve, but that's life. They weren't traumas to bookend other ones."

"I don't have any traumas." He refused to admit anything that had happened to him was a trauma. It was life, too.

"Everything you just told me about your father, what little I knew about him in the first place, that's a trauma. What happened with your sister? It's a tragedy. Your tragedy."

"It's just life. Same as yours. Susannah saved me. That's all that mattered."

"No." Pen shook her head. "You can't ignore those traumas. You think you can erase your beginnings, but—"

"You're damn right I can erase them," he exploded, jerking away from her touch. From her. "Those first thirteen years don't exist. I don't think about them. It's nothing to me. My life started when Susannah brought me into this house."

Tears were shining in her eyes, but they didn't fall. "But that isn't true, no matter how much we all want it to be. Those years were your foundation. They're part of who you are. You can't build your life without a foundation. Good or bad."

"I did. I do." And that was it. He had. He would continue to do so. "I told you the truth. It's not my problem if you can't believe it."

"Ethan—"

But he was done. Let it prove her point to *her*. He knew the truth. He was protecting her and her girls. He didn't care enough about himself to protect himself.

Chapter Fourteen

"How you feeling, kiddo?" Dad asked, poking his head in Pen's bedroom door.

Pen looked up from where she was sitting on her floor, frowning at the terrible wrapping job everyone in her family had done for the Santa presents she'd have to smuggle downstairs after the girls went to bed.

"Close the door," she instructed.

He did so, stepping inside her room and closing the door.

"They're not going to think Santa did this."

"Well, I guess you should've taught Sadie or Mack how to wrap better."

"Neither of them will listen to me. Then or now." Pen sighed. Maybe it was silly to worry about something as foolish as wrapping paper. Addie might notice, but Brynn and Daisy would be too excited about presents and candy.

"Wrapping wasn't quite what I meant when I asked how you were feeling."

"My arm is fine."

"Pen."

She looked at her father then, really looked at him. He

looked...sad. Which she didn't understand.

His expression turned sheepish and he cleared his throat. "I may have overheard a few things this morning."

"Oh." Her father had listened to her argue with Ethan. "Oh."

"Not the whole thing. Mostly the tail end. Right before he busted out of there."

"Right, well. I feel...sore. Heart sore. But I can't..." She sucked in a breath and the one she let out was shaky. It wasn't easy to admit, but she was getting there. "I can't make him deal with things he doesn't want to deal with. I can't make him admit to feelings he doesn't want to feel."

"It never occurred to me. That he might be so torn up."

"Don't feel guilty, Dad. It never occurred to me either. Not until this past month and dealing with my issues about Mom. It only made sense in my own context. He's very good at acting, at pretending."

"Apparently. He's too smart to not see it for truth. Stubborn enough it might take some time, but you'll get through to him."

Pen wished she could believe that as wholeheartedly as Dad seemed to. She knew it was possible, but part of her wondered if she had what it took. "Thanks. I just want to try and enjoy Christmas." She rubbed at her chest. Her heart really did hurt, but she was accustomed to good and hurt existing in the same day. The same second. She'd deal and handle both.

"For what it's worth, I..." He cleared his throat again,

clearly dealing with a bigger emotion than he was letting on. "You sounded like her. The way she would have fought. The way she fought for me a time or two. She would have been very proud of a great many things you've done and survived in your life, Pen, but she would have been especially proud of that."

Pen stood, doing her best to blink back tears since she knew how uncomfortable they made her father. Still, she wrapped him in a tight hug. "Thank you, Daddy."

Dad grunted and awkwardly patted her back, which made her smile. She pulled away on a deep breath.

"I need to go help Sadie with dinner. Get the girls to wash up."

"Mack and Colt were helping. Brack was rounding up the girls. All we need is you."

Pen smiled. "Me, you've got." She reached for the door, but it was opening before she managed to get there.

Sadie poked in looking oddly frazzled.

"Pen. We…we can't find Addie."

There was a moment where those words together didn't make any sense. She could only stare at Sadie and feel utterly and wholly dumb. "What do you mean?"

"We've looked everywhere. The girls haven't seen her since this morning." Sadie wrung her hands together. "I checked on her at lunch but her door was locked and she told me to go away."

"Me too."

"Her door isn't locked anymore. She's not in her room,

and we've started looking all over, but there's no sign of her."

Pen swallowed at the swift kick of panic. "She was angry. She's hiding. Trying to scare us. That's all."

Sadie nodded, but she noted her sister didn't look any more convinced than Pen herself felt. Addie had tried to hitch a ride home from the parade. Pen had been so wrapped up in her own stuff, so sure Addie would grow out of these moods and random bouts of saying she hated it here.

"Why don't you come check her room with me?" Sadie said, taking Pen's arm. "Dad, you know the land better. Take the Gator out."

Dad was moving out the door before Sadie finished the sentence. Sadie pulled Pen into the hallway.

"You can't start blaming yourself before we even know what's going on," Sadie said brusquely. But Pen knew her sister well enough to know that brusque was trying to hide panic and fear.

"I haven't been listening to her."

"She's twelve. Which isn't to say you shouldn't listen to her, but you can't take every snotty comment to heart. Especially not when you're dealing with your own stuff. Addie gets mad and she acts out, but most days she's happy. Here and with us. You know that."

Pen wanted to know that, but she wasn't so certain she did. She stepped into Addie and Brynn's room. It was its usual mess—a mishmash of the opposite interests her girls had. But the first thing Pen noticed was that Henry's picture was missing.

"She ran away. Really ran away." Pen started pawing through her messy, unmade bed. The bear with a police uniform and Henry's name stitched on it that each of the girls had gotten was gone too. "She's taken all Henry's stuff. She seriously ran away." Pen stood for a brief second completely frozen by panic. "She ran away."

"Call Ethan. On the crazy off chance she got off the property, he'll know what to do."

Pen shook her head, her hands shaking as she dug her phone out of her pocket. "He won't answer a call from me."

"Fine." Sadie pulled out her own phone and held it to her ear. Presumably Ethan answered, but Sadie didn't even pause for a hello.

"Addie ran away." After a moment, Sadie held out the phone to her. "He said he needs to talk to you."

With nerveless fingers, Pen took the phone. "Ethan?"

"Call dispatch with a description and answer all their questions. Make sure you tell them you're her mother. They'll put out the official alert. Keep looking on the property. There's a lot of places to hide, and almost always in missing kids' cases they're just in the house. It'd be awfully hard for her to get all the way out here, but we'll make sure. You go on and call dispatch. I'll text you the number, okay?"

"Ethan..."

"Then call all of her friends and ask them if they know anything. Relay any information to me or dispatch. We'll find her, Pen. I promise."

Ethan might pretend, he might be mad at her or whatever, but Pen had to believe that promise.

EVERY SECOND THAT ticked by without word on Addie made the thing that had been wrapped around Ethan's lungs all day tighter. Deadlier.

He didn't know how she would have gotten off the property. She had to be on the farm. But they hadn't found her yet.

Where would a twelve-year-old go?

When he'd wanted to escape his home, he'd tried getting in trouble. But that was because he hadn't been loved. He wasn't running from…whatever Addie was running from. The argument with Brynn. What he'd said to her about doing it out of meanness. Something bigger. Something smaller. She was running from an event.

He'd been running from a prison sentence.

Hadn't Mack run away once when she'd been really little? When Fritz had still been struggling with Susannah's death. They'd found her in town somewhere…at the bus station?

Ethan did an illegal U-turn and headed for the bus station. The buses didn't run this late on Christmas Eve, and the outside depot was mostly open. It was dark except for the security lights, and under those lights was a small lump on a bench outside the depot.

He nearly fell to his knees in thanks, but worry and some

shade of horror had him parking and jumping out of his cruiser. He texted Pen quickly as he strode toward Addie.

When Addie heard him coming, she scowled. "Go away."

"Addie. You've got everyone frantically searching for you. I'm not going away. I've already told your mom I found you."

"I want to go home."

"I'll take you home."

"No. Not that stupid place. San Antonio. My old house. I want to go home and see my dad and have everything go back to the way it was and I don't want to ever see you again."

"Me?"

"I hate you! I hate you the most. I hate…" She had big tears rolling down her cheeks and she just broke down into sobs. "Why don't you want us?"

Ethan could only stare. "Addie, I don't know what you're talking about."

Her head whipped up, desolation turning to fury in five seconds flat. "You said if Mom didn't have us, you would be with her, but you couldn't handle her three kids."

"That isn't what…" Christ. Had he said that? It wasn't what he'd meant, but if she'd been eavesdropping she could have misconstrued. "Addie, that's all out of context. I didn't say it like that. I don't mean it like that."

"I don't care. Context is stupid. You're stupid. Everything is stupid and I want my old life back."

"I know you do. But it's gone."

Which he only realized was the worst possible thing to say when she started sobbing in earnest. He picked her up and sat on the bench, pulling her into his lap. He held her while she cried and wondered how any mother could do *this*.

Have your heart ripped to shreds because there was nothing you could do to take that pain away for a child. He just had to hold her while she felt it.

He sucked in a sharp breath. Because here he was, heart ripped to shreds and holding her while she cried and…simply surviving. Because it was the only choice. Because it was about helping her, not the pain it caused him.

She sniffled and wiped her cheeks, slowly getting a hold of herself. But she stayed on his lap, curled against him.

"How did you get out here?"

"Cathy's brother drove us over to the bakery." She sniffled, her head snuggled into his shoulder. "Then Cathy told him my mom picked me up while he was gone."

"Do you have any idea of how dangerous that was? To be here alone? No phone. No money."

Her head popped up. "I have money! But all the buses were gone by the time I got here."

"Would you have really done that?"

"I have friends in San Antonio. I could have stayed with one of them. I made a plan. Ever since we moved here."

"Addie. I… Do you know how badly this is going to hurt your mother?"

Her chin wobbled but she didn't start crying again.

"Maybe she would have been better off. Maybe two girls wouldn't be so hard for *you*." She said it snottily, but it shook him how much of this was about him. About what he'd said to Pen that he'd never meant Addie to overhear.

"You misunderstood me, Addie. Completely." He didn't want to tell her about his father. It was too complicated and the last thing he wanted to do was scare her. "I was just trying to protect you from some…hard things. I was telling your mom I didn't want to drag you four into it. I didn't want to hurt you. So, I was going to stay away from… I just thought it would be better to be alone."

Telling it to a twelve-year-old, hearing it echo there between him, something inside of him shifted. With Addie on his lap he finally realized…

He wouldn't let his father touch her. Not her or Brynn or Daisy. Not Fritz. Not Pen or Mack or Sadie. And Colt and Bracken would stand right beside him to make sure that didn't happen.

He'd do whatever it took, just like Susannah had for him once upon a time. He knew that in his soul.

Which made everything Pen had said to him this morning feel…all that more convicting.

"If it's a hard thing, a scary thing, you're not supposed to run away from it. You're supposed to ask for help."

Ethan was rendered frozen and mute. How many times had Susannah said that to him in their short time together? "Who told you that?" he choked out.

She shrugged. "No one exactly. Daddy used to say he

was a helper, so there was never any shame asking for help. And Mom would tell him she wasn't *ashamed*, she just didn't want to. But he was right."

It almost made Ethan smile since it was such a patently Pen thing to say. But he looked at the girl in his lap, a girl he'd die for without question. He would do that, but he wouldn't give himself over fully to that feeling? He'd act, but he wouldn't give?

"I guess I need help then." From a twelve-year-old? What was wrong with him?

"With what?"

"I'm afraid." He wasn't sure he'd ever admitted that to anyone, but Addie looked up at him with new consideration in her eyes.

"Of what?"

"That your mom was right. That all the reasons I had for turning away from my heart were because I was afraid of what I was feeling. Not because of all the reasons I made up in my head."

"I hate when she's right."

"Yeah. She is more often than not."

"I guess," Addie grumbled.

"You didn't ask her for help," Ethan pointed out. "You've been planning to run away, but you haven't told her. You haven't asked her to help you get through your feelings. You had to know this would hurt her."

"Sometimes it hurts so much inside me I just want to make it hurt for everyone else. I'm supposed to write in my journal." She rolled her eyes.

Ethan nodded. Even though he hadn't felt that way, that had been Bracken before Susannah had died.

But Susannah had saved them, changed them in life and then in death.

He didn't need to save or change Addie, but maybe he could still help. By doing something he'd never done with anyone, not even the people he loved. Actually...talk. About feelings. "You know, I don't think I ever really dealt with your grandma dying. I know you didn't know her, but she was a mother to me. She meant a lot to me. And a lot like your dad, she died kind of suddenly when it felt like we really needed her."

"We did need him," Addie whispered.

"But see, you lost him. I know that's hard. I've lost Susannah and I lost my sister. I thought there was something I could have done to change it, but there's not really. Life can be a little mean." He thought of what Pen had said about life hurting, which is why you had to let the love in. "But if you're lucky, you have a really great family who loves you. And when you lose someone, you all work together to help each other. Love each other. You have that family, Addie. I know you know that."

"I didn't mean to hurt Brynn's feelings this morning," she whispered. "I just didn't want to see her disappointed."

"See? You were trying to protect her, just like parents try to protect their kids. But it's hard sometimes to know how to do it, and people don't always appreciate it. And sometimes..." Ethan took a deep breath to try to ease the tightening in his throat. "Sometimes we tell ourselves we're protecting someone we love, but what we're really doing is protecting ourselves."

"Maybe. I don't like... I don't want to hope for good things, but I hoped for you. And then...you said..."

He closed his eyes, amazed the waves of pain could keep coming and he could get through them. Talk through them. But he had to. For Addie.

"I love you, Addie. No choice I ever make would change that. Nothing I ever say should make you think otherwise. And I'll work very hard to make sure I don't."

She nodded solemnly.

"I need a promise from you now."

"No more running away," she grumbled. She let out a gusty sigh. "I just... Everything hurt. I didn't want to feel that way. I wanted to get away from it."

How well he understood that. But he'd never run away from the Martins. No, that was too big a sacrifice. So he'd held himself back and separate. Because he didn't want to feel that way—whatever way it was.

"You know, a long time ago your grandma told me I should ask for help. I didn't listen, but I'm going to try to listen to you, okay? And I want you to know, you can always ask me for help. Always."

She watched him very seriously. "Are you in love with my mom?"

He could have given her a lot of answers, but with all this

pain inside of him, he only had the truth. "Yes."

"Are you going to be with her? Like...Cathy's mom has a boyfriend. But they're getting married."

Ethan rubbed a hand over his face. "I don't... I don't know."

"You should. You make her happy. She should be happy." She seemed to think it over for a minute. "And you should be happy. If you love her, you're supposed to be together."

"Even if it means you have to stay at the farm and not move back to San Antonio?"

Addie shrugged. "I guess."

"I don't know what's going to happen between me and your mom, Addie, but whatever it is, I promise—I'm part of your life, part of your family. So, no more eavesdropping. No more thinking the worst of what you hear without talking it out, deal?"

She nodded reluctantly.

He stood, gently placing her on her feet. "All right. Now, I've got to get you home."

"Mom's going to be mad," Addie replied, looking at his cruiser dubiously.

"Very," he agreed. "But you're going to ask for help. And you're going to tell her how you feel. Your mom loves you no matter what."

"I know." Addie slid her hand in his. "I love you, Ethan."

If that wasn't the final nail in his coffin, he didn't know what would be.

Chapter Fifteen

PEN NEARLY LEAPT out the door when she heard the engine. She knew better than to believe anyone was actually asleep, but everyone had left her to deal with Addie one on one once they'd heard she was safe.

Luckily Daisy and Brynn were easily distracted by Christmas cookies and tales of Santa, so while they might have had some idea of what was going on, they hadn't been overly interested. They'd fallen asleep after sugar crashes, ready to wake up to Christmas morning.

Pen stepped out into Christmas Eve night and tried to remind herself it was a season to be forgiving.

Ethan stepped out of his cruiser, his uniform looking so *menacing* as he helped her firstborn out of the car. The lights didn't make it look festive or sweet. It looked like doom.

But that was an overreaction. Addie was safe. The end.

Addie trudged toward the porch, Ethan following at a distance.

"Adelaide Susannah Wakefield. I don't even know how to describe how much trouble you're in," Pen managed, though her voice wavered and the second Addie was close enough Pen grabbed her and held on. "Baby. You scared me to death."

Addie didn't say anything, but she made the choking sound she always did when she was trying not to cry.

Pen finally managed to release her. "You go on up to my room. I'll be up in a second to have a talk with you."

Addie didn't argue, and she didn't stomp off but moved away quietly. She'd clearly been crying either with Ethan or before he'd found her. Pen closed her eyes for a minute, prayed to find the right way to handle all this.

"She was at the bus station?" she managed to ask Ethan.

"She schemed with her friend Cathy. So, that's a conversation you might want to have with Cathy's parents."

Pen nodded. The weight of parenthood never got lighter. It just shifted into different hard things she never quite saw coming. "She's okay," Pen said, more to herself than for any other reason.

"She is. We talked a little. She…" Ethan cleared his throat. "She was mostly mad at me. Catching her fighting with Brynn this morning then she… Well, she overheard some things this morning."

It was wrong to be relieved Addie's issues were geared more toward Ethan than her, than living on the farm, but boy was she.

"I should have been more careful."

"Pen—"

"Thank you," she said, cutting him off. "For finding her. I can't… Thank you."

He didn't say anything, although the way he looked at

her didn't make any sense. "You don't have to. I'll always help."

Which seemed to mean *I'll always stay right here, within touching distance but just out of reach.* She didn't have the energy to fight that now. She'd deal with Ethan…well, not tomorrow since he never came over on Christmas. The day after. It'd give her time to build up her fight again.

She turned back to the house. She had to face Addie without tears and without yelling. She had to be calm. She had to get to the bottom of this.

She climbed the stairs, and when she opened the door to her room, Addie was sitting in the middle of Pen's bed staring out the window, the Henry teddy bear in her lap.

"What you did today was incredibly dangerous, and you're so lucky nothing bad happened to you. I know Last Stand is safe, but that was irresponsible. Your father taught you much better than that."

"I miss him."

Pen's heart cracked. She held on to her control as best she could, but the chances of getting through this without crying were slim. "I do too. I think we always will. There's nothing wrong about missing someone. It means you loved them very much. Which means…" She couldn't tell her daughter whose father had been shot in the line of duty that she was *lucky*. No matter how good love was, losing someone didn't make having them lucky. "It's okay to be sad. You deserve to be sad sometimes."

"Sometimes when I miss him, I just want to be mad.

And mean."

"Maybe we should find a counselor here like we had back in San Antonio. Someone you can talk to and—"

"Mom, no. I don't want to. It's weird to talk to someone I don't know. I don't like it. I... Please, Mom. I promise. I'll talk. I just...don't always want to talk to you. But not a doctor. I promise to talk to Grandpa or...Aunt Sadie. Please."

"Of course. They're your family. But I need your word. Your *promise* that you'll do that. If anything even remotely like this happens ever again, not only will you be going to therapy, you will have so many extra chores as well. Therapy is to help you. Chores are a punishment."

Addie nodded. "I promise." She bit her lip and looked down at her lap. "Mom, I'm sorry I scared you. I wasn't thinking about you."

"I know." Pen thought it was quite the feat Addie understood and acknowledged that. "Try to remember we all love you and want the best for you. Always. No matter what. And if it doesn't feel that way, you only have to tell us. I can't give you everything you want, Addie. Sometimes what we want isn't possible, or isn't what we need, but I'm always doing my best for you and your sisters."

"Brynn wants you to get married again, and I... I wouldn't mind. Depending. But it made me miss Dad. Brynn and Daisy...they don't remember him like I do. They don't..."

"But I do." The first tear slid over and Pen slid onto her

bed next to Addie. "And I'm right here."

"I don't want to make you sad."

"If you're sad, it's okay to make me sad. We'll be sad together. And if we're sad together, we can get back to being happy. Because we have each other."

Addie seemed to take that on board. But then she changed the subject altogether. "Do you love Ethan?"

"Huh?"

"I asked him if he loved you."

Pen opened her mouth, but the last thing she was going to do was ask her twelve-year-old what he'd said.

"He said he did. And he said he's been afraid." Addie frowned. "I think he needs..." She seemed to struggle to come up with the words, and Pen couldn't blame her. "I guess he just needs us."

"I think so," Pen said, her throat tightening all over again.

"We'll need to talk to him then," Addie said with all the seriousness of an adult who knew just what to do. "So he can be happy too. When he's done being sad."

"Yes, we'll talk to him. But not tonight. You need sleep."

"I could help with Santa. I feel bad that I... I could help."

Pen opened her mouth to argue, but she realized Addie had made the suggestion both as peace offering but also because she wanted to. So, Pen nodded. "All right. But don't think you're getting off that easy. The remainder of your winter break you are on goat poop duty."

Addie's face fell into disgust and horror. "But—"

"That's just the beginning, young lady. You ran away. You could have..." She couldn't bear to tell Addie all the horrible scenarios that had gone through her mind while she'd been frantically searching. "The punishment is big. And smelly."

Addie grumbled, but Pen managed a smile. Things would be okay. Being the mother of this girl was never going to be *easy*, but it was amazing.

ETHAN GOT OFF work, ran through the shower, and got dressed in jeans and a T-shirt. He didn't work again until evening. Which meant he had all day to do his usual grave visiting.

Except he'd changed his plans last night after dropping Addie off.

Usually he only went and put flowers on Amy's grave. He never said anything, aloud or in his head. He just placed the flowers on her grave, cleaned up around if it needed it, and moved on.

It felt like a penance, not a visit. He'd always preferred that. Because penance he could control. Grief...not so much.

Which meant something had to change. Not with his sister, because as much as he'd loved her, she hadn't been an integral part of his life. She'd been the cautionary tale, the catalyst.

But Susannah had been his mother, in every way that counted. And he hadn't been to her grave since the funeral.

Everything inside of him rebelled against doing so this morning. He'd always listened to that. Called it his gut feeling.

But he couldn't stop turning over Addie's runaway attempt in his mind. What if she'd gone through with it? What if something had happened to her? And all because she was running away from feelings everyone around her would understand, would listen to.

He had all those same people. People who loved him and wanted the best for him. Who didn't want him on the periphery. They'd let him be because he hadn't been honest, but Pen had seen through it.

He had to own up to that.

So he drove to the cemetery in the dark Christmas morning. He parked in the lot, preferring to walk to the site rather than drive through. He noted two odd shadows in the distance near Susannah's grave. He stopped abruptly as he realized the two shadows were men. Both turned to face him.

"You don't usually come here," Bracken offered by way of greeting.

"No, I don't," Ethan replied, forcing himself to take the remaining steps to Colt and Bracken. And Susannah. "Do you?"

"Colt and I always do Christmas morning. We used to invite you, but you always said no. Usually come out a little later in the day. You know, daylight and not freezing, but

Colt wanted to be back to the farm for Santa." Bracken leaned forward as if letting Ethan in on a secret. "Getting kid ideas."

"I... I haven't been here since the funeral."

Bracken and Colt exchanged a look.

It was dark and cold, but here were his brothers if not by blood by everything else. His brothers, who he could talk to. Even about feelings.

Colt handed him a couple flowers from the bunch in his hand and all three of them kneeled to lay them at the base of the gravestone.

Ethan looked at that smooth stone with Susannah's name carved on it, dates underneath. He'd had to accept she was gone—there was no pretending she wasn't. But he hadn't let himself feel the pain of that without trying to push it into something else.

"So." Colt rocked back on his heels. "This mean what it should mean?"

Ethan straightened. "What should it mean?"

"That you're going to finally live."

"I've been living just fine," he grumbled, even knowing it was a lie. Even knowing he'd come here to stop lying. But Rome wasn't built in a day and he had a hell of a lot of building to do.

"There's a difference between surviving and living, Ethan." Colt gave Bracken a pointed look as if to say, *for you too, buddy*. "Living can be a little harder, but it's always a hell of a lot sweeter. Takes a bit of courage though. And usually a

Martin woman to knock some sense into you."

"If I recall, my fist also knocked some sense into you."

Colt laughed at the memory of their fight when Colt had been trying to run away—from the farm, from Sadie and Fritz. From everything.

"I started that, though. You never would have punched first."

No. And he'd never run away. He'd just always do the thing that didn't require action, didn't require feeling. He looked at Susannah's name. "She had more courage than anyone I've ever known. Never backed down. That should have been what I internalized. How to be brave, like her. Instead I... I've kept myself separate."

"It took me a long time to believe in what she saw in me." Colt was silent for a few minutes. "Maybe three morons like us need a little love before we can be brave."

"Morons like you two," Bracken replied grimly. "I'll stay out of your insanity, thank you."

"Except I'm marrying Sadie. Ethan's going to grovel to Pen." Colt looked at Bracken and grinned. "Who's that leave you?"

Bracken lifted a middle finger, but didn't say anything else.

"I never said I was going to grovel," Ethan finally said. He was going to...talk. They were going to have a conversation about feelings, as horrible as that sounded. He wasn't going to beg.

Hopefully.

"Boy, you better," Colt said slapping him on the back.

"You just sounded exactly like Fritz," Bracken said with a mock shudder. "That's creepy."

"Better than sounding like my old man."

"No," Ethan said, still staring at Susannah's name. "Fritz is our old man. Susannah was our mother. They're our real parents." Because Fritz and Susannah had always given them what parents were supposed to. Whatever each of their biological parents might have done to scar them, Fritz and Susannah had done what they could to heal those scars.

"Damn right."

Bracken nodded in agreement.

"It's hard to miss her when we didn't have her long enough." He knew his voice came out scratchy, and that the bald emotion didn't make any of them comfortable. But they still stood here. Together. Listening.

"Long enough to matter, though," Colt replied, his voice raspy too.

Ethan and Bracken nodded in unison, then they took an unplanned collective breath together. Together in front of their mother, who'd given them everything they'd needed.

Now Ethan had to be brave enough to do something with it.

"You ready?" Colt asked.

Ethan nodded and they turned away from Susannah's grave together. Because they were family, because of her.

"So, you figured out how to grovel yet?" Bracken asked as they reached where Colt had parked his truck.

"Just one part."

"What's that?" Colt asked.

"Show up for Christmas."

"That'll be a first," Bracken said.

Ethan nodded. "Yeah. A lot of firsts."

Chapter Sixteen

PEN YAWNED AS she peeked into the living room to make sure everything was as she'd left it. It was still dark out, but she always set her alarm to wake up before the girls so she could see their faces.

But there weren't just presents under the colorful tree. No, Ethan was crouched there, putting new presents in with the others.

For a moment she thought to convince herself it was a dream. She'd barely slept after all the worry over Addie. She was hallucinating.

But he stood slowly, turning to face her.

Her heart seemed to jump into her throat, hammer there instead of her chest. She couldn't get her hopes up and think this meant something. But it was Christmas and he was *here*.

"What are you doing?" she asked, sounding as shaken as she felt.

"I had some presents to put under the tree."

"That isn't what I meant and you know it." Irritation steadied her. "You're here. On Christmas."

"I'm here. On Christmas."

She wanted to say something. Anything. But all she

could do was stand there and stare at him in the dim room. It was that eerie quiet before a storm of noise and activity. Dawn was just beginning to creep into the windows and the white lights on the tree made Ethan glow.

But he didn't say anything, and she didn't know what else to say to him. She'd said it all. Over and over again. She couldn't *make* him understand. He had to want to.

"I went to Susannah's grave this morning."

"With Colt and Bracken?"

He shook his head. "No. I mean, they were there, but I didn't know they would be."

She stared at him in confusion. "They always go. I thought…" How silly she'd been to think he'd do something that required him to face his feelings.

"I never go. I'd refused so much they stopped asking and I forgot they even did it. My usual Christmas tradition aside from work is go to my sister's grave and beat myself up over all the ways I've failed."

"That doesn't sound very festive."

"No, but it's rather satisfying. Because it ignores grief. It ignores sadness and turns it into self-pity, but the kind you get to feel self-righteous about."

"I might know a thing or two about that. Not the guilt thing, but the self-righteous thing."

"Yeah. I figure that's why you weren't exactly…wrong yesterday."

"You really need to work on your groveling."

"I'm not…" He let out a sigh. "I don't know how to

grovel. I don't know how to do any of this."

"But you're here." She managed to smile at him. "On Christmas."

"Yes. On Christmas."

He smiled, and she didn't know how to read it. It was sad, but not heavy. He seemed calm—quiet but not detached. She didn't know how to *read* him and it was driving her a little insane.

"I went to Susannah's grave because I hadn't, and I figured I needed to. And maybe part of me was hoping I'd be fine and prove you wrong."

"But you weren't."

"Colt and Brack were there and…" He shook his head. "They loved her too. They lost her too. We all did. We're all trying to figure out how to maneuver it. You've been doing that. I didn't want to. I still don't *want* to."

"Why not?"

"Susannah was the only person I've ever said I love you to. And it was too late. She was already gone when I finally said the words."

She moved toward him but he held up a hand and she stopped on a dime. Maybe…this wasn't what she'd hoped it would be.

"I didn't want to hurt like that again. I didn't ever want to hurt like that again. If you put a wall between yourself and it, you don't have to… It isn't devastating."

"But then you're alone, which is."

Ethan nodded. "Colt asked me if I was ready to start living. I thought I was. I go to work. I help out here. I'm *here* and I wake up every morning—how is that not living?" He shook his head. "But I've been surviving, trying to sidestep all the ways life can knock you on your ass. Being alone is a pain I understand. It's a pain I'm used to—since I was a kid. But I couldn't seem to function through the pain of losing the first person I truly loved unreservedly. So, I thought I put it away, but I guess I put myself away. Regressed back to someone waiting for the world to fall apart and trying to avoid getting hurt by that."

"So, what are you going to do?"

"I'm not sure I know how to be something different, but I want to try. With you. And your girls. Well, with everyone, but you four in particular."

What Pen really wanted to do was leap into his arms. To figure the rest out later. To hold on to *try*.

But she was an adult, with three kids. She had to be… She had to be sensible. "What about your father and all that stuff about him being a threat when he's released?"

"As I sat there talking to Addie at the bus station, it struck me that it didn't matter. It didn't matter if I was in your life or not because I'd do anything, sacrifice anything, to keep you all safe. We'd all do that for each other. I knew that, but I had it all…twisted in my head. I needed to see… Well, I guess I needed a real reason to make it click."

"A 'you were right, Pen' would go a long way here."

His smile widened. He might have even chuckled. He also stepped toward her. "You were right, Pen." He stopped right in front of her. So close. And when he touched her, it was featherlight, the backs of his fingers against her cheek. "I love you."

She felt her heart stutter to a stop. He was so certain. So *here*. "I know."

"YOU..." THAT WAS not exactly what Ethan had expected to hear the first time he said that to someone who was conscious and among the living. "You know?"

She grinned up at him. "Addie told me."

He laughed, and it was strange. His heart hurt, but it was lighter than it had been. He was sad, but there was a happiness buoying that sadness up. "I've got my work cut out for me, don't I?"

"You have no idea."

He figured neither did she, but they'd figure it out together. For the first time he understood that word. Together. The weight of it. The importance of it. Why it was worth the potential for loss. "A very long time ago your mother told me you had a crush on me."

"And you thought I was repulsive," she returned, wrinkling her nose.

"No. I was scared, because she told me I wouldn't be the boy for you until I learned to deal with my demons. I just wanted to ignore them. I just wanted them to not exist. So, I decided I wouldn't be the boy for you, and I would put all those demons away. Make them not exist. But they existed inside of me, even when I didn't give them any light. That little boy who had a manipulative father and a mother who supported that man no matter who he hurt—he was there. Making decisions an adult should have been making. But you were wrong about one thing."

She sniffed, lifting her chin. "I doubt that very much," she said haughtily. Tears in her eyes, smile tugging her lips.

The combination of deep emotions he'd been avoiding so long he hadn't even known he was doing it and her smile felt like a lock clicking open. It was a change, all the smaller changes leading up to this moment unleashed this big one.

"I don't need those first thirteen years as foundation—yeah, they happened and yes, I need to face them and deal with them when they inform my choices, but the foundation I built my life on is the one Susannah gave me. I made some bad choices along the way, but she gave me all of you. She saved me, much as she could. Now I have to do the rest of the saving."

Pen swallowed audibly and blinked rapidly. "Well," she said, her voice cracking before she shook her hair back, pinning him with a regal expression. "Are you ever going to kiss me? Or are we going to talk ourselves to death until the girls wake up?"

"Are you sure... Are you sure you want to take all this on?"

"I have three daughters. Your baggage has *nothing* on what you're taking on."

He cupped her face, looked her right in the eye. He knew he'd have to get used to doing just this. Over and over again. "I love you. I love them." Then he did what he should have done a long time ago and kissed her.

And let himself go. Fully. Wholly. Knowing she would always hold his heart. Knowing it would be hard, but there'd be this. That no matter what happened, no matter what hurt, her love would fill up the cracks life created.

Brynn's screech pierced the air and Pen jerked away in surprise, but then leaned in to him as she saw the girls standing in the threshold of the living room.

Brynn had a look of absolute awe on her face. "Santa *did* it!" she whispered.

"What?" Pen looked at her daughter in confusion. "Santa did what?"

Addie grinned at Ethan and slid her arm around Brynn's shoulder. "He really did."

Pen looked up at him. "What on earth am I missing?"

Ethan shook his head, though he couldn't help grinning back at Addie. "Nothing. You're not missing a thing."

Brynn rushed forward, throwing herself at both of them. "Are you guys gonna get married? Is Ethan gonna sleep in your bed?"

Ethan might have choked on his own spit over that one, but Brynn was already bouncing away. "Look at all these *presents*!"

Pen laughed as the girls started poking through looking for their names. She hooked her arm around his waist. "Still sure?"

"Always." Because Ethan Thompson's greatest secret had been revealed. His secrets. His lies.

And now his life could really begin—on the foundation Susannah had given him, and on the love Pen had convinced him to feel.

Epilogue

Nine months later

"BUT I HATE math."

Brynn's whining had put Pen on considerable edge. Especially since she knew if Brynn spent even half the time trying to figure it out that she spent complaining about math, homework would take half as long.

And since Fritz and Sadie were *cowards* and always disappeared once the homework came out, Pen was left to deal.

She hadn't been dealing very well tonight. Then Ethan had taken over when he'd gotten home. He'd slid into what had become *his* seat. She put the dinner she'd saved for him next to his elbow, and he'd set about working with Brynn through her math homework while he ate his dinner.

He wasn't a perfect man, but he sure knew how to make a perfect moment, his head together with Brynn's, helping her through a frustrating concept.

It was just a shame she was tired of…just this. He'd been staying at the farm since Christmas, but insisted on keeping separate rooms *for the sake of the girls.*

Pen rolled her eyes at that.

All of his worries about his father's retribution had turned out to be...pointless seemed a harsh word, but not only had Ethan's police friends kept an eye on Abe Thompson, the whole town had. The first time Abe had stepped foot into Last Stand, Minna Herdmann—the town's matriarch—had immediately called the police and told them to keep an eye on that man.

The one and only time Abe had even tried to head out toward the farm, one of the other police officers had pulled him over. Abe had lost it and was thankfully back in jail after his altercation with the officer.

Though she knew Ethan felt somewhat guilty other people were involved, he'd learned an invaluable lesson about how many people loved him and would help keep him and the Martins safe.

Things were good. Settled. Sadie's agritourism plan was taking off like gangbusters and Pen had found herself enjoying giving people tours in a way she didn't enjoy milking or cheese making. Ethan came home and helped with homework and said I love you to all of them, sincerely and often.

But Colt had finished up the cabin Ethan had agreed to let him build. Ethan could move in whenever he wanted. He'd said something about getting it furnished first, but he hadn't said anything about what came next.

If he moved out to that cabin without even bringing up her and the girls moving with him, she'd knock him out with a frying pan. Or so she told herself in the privacy of her own head.

"Finished! Finally. Mom, can I—"

"It's fifteen minutes past your bedtime. Brush teeth. Go to bed."

Brynn groaned dramatically. "That's not fair."

"I know. It's cruel and unusual. Just like your whining."

"Ughhhh." The sound continued as Brynn slowly, slowly, stomped her way up the stairs.

"I don't know how I'm going to survive fourth grade math," Ethan said around a yawn. "I don't think I survived it the first time around."

Him. How *he* was going to survive it. Because he was a part of this. A part of this and doing *nothing* to make that permanent.

Pen tossed the dishrag into the sink and whirled. "When are you going to ask me to marry you?"

He looked like a deer caught in headlights before he slowly closed Brynn's math book. He didn't say anything. Forever.

It was his great superpower, because as much as his quietness before had been about holding himself separate, Ethan was a naturally *careful* man. He didn't let her start stupid fights—too often—because he took his time. He thought about what he said before he said it.

She loved him for all of those things even if she currently wanted to shake him until words fell out. Of course, when they did, they always inevitably shocked *her* into silence.

"October sixteenth."

She'd expected a hedge. Or maybe a question to turn it around on her. *When do you want me to ask you to marry me?* Or worse some horrible secret about never wanting to get married.

But he'd given her a date. A very specific date. "October... Be serious."

He stood in that slow, careful way of his. "I'm very serious. I'm going to ask you to marry me on October sixteenth."

"Why would you..." It dawned on her then, what that date meant. "Mom's birthday."

He shrugged. He was trying to act casual, but he was uncomfortable. "Susannah brought me into your life, I figured it'd be symbolic."

She teared up just from him thinking such a thing. "Oh, damn you."

"When you start cursing me I know I really did something right." He slid his arms around her waist.

She let herself lean in to his chest. He'd made that easy. The leaning. The partnership. Life wasn't easy, and he wasn't who she'd once thought he'd been, but he was her dependable Ethan. She knew she could always lean, trust, believe.

"I have to wait another month. What for?" She looked up at him, an idea occurring to her. She grinned.

"That smile is always scary, I hope you know."

"I do. I think it's well established I don't mind scaring you a little bit. Sometimes you need it."

"I suppose I do."

"I don't want to wait, but I do want a special date like that. We could get *married* on October sixteenth."

"But that's only a month away."

"So? We elope. I don't want a big wedding—I already did that. And you don't strike me as a man who really wants to get dressed up and profess his love for me in front of everyone we know."

He shuddered. "You want to just…elope?"

"Well, the girls would have to be there. And Dad. Well…okay, the family would have to be there. But nothing big. Nothing fancy. Just all of us and a promise."

"And love."

She rose onto her toes to kiss him, but he stopped her. "Wait a second. Did you just…ruin my proposal?" he asked in mock horror.

"I didn't ruin it. It was your idea. I just…enhanced it."

He laughed, tucking a strand of hair behind her ear. "Sounds about right." When she tried to kiss him again, he stopped her.

She scowled at him, but he only smiled. "Wait right here."

"Wait for what?"

But he didn't answer her. He disappeared upstairs. When he returned he held a velvet box.

"You have a ring." He had a *ring*. Somehow that made it crystalize. What she was doing. What she was promising. All she wanted, and how lucky she was to be able to reach out for it.

"Sit down."

"But—"

He gave her what she liked to call his *cop* look. Authoritative. He didn't bring it out very often, but it was *very* effective. She sat down.

He got down on one knee in front of her. "I can't have people saying you proposed to me now, can I?" He took her hand. "I love you. You saved me from the dark place I'd grown accustomed to. I want you by my side, forever. So, Penelope, will you marry me? Apparently in one month."

She laughed. She cried. She slid off the chair and grabbed on to him. For a few seconds she didn't even look at the ring, she just held on to him. Grateful for him. For the life she'd been given. "You saved me too, you know. Maybe not as dramatically. But you've always made it easy to lean on you, when I don't think it's easy to lean on anyone. You gave me that. So, yes, I'll marry you. In one month."

He pulled away and slid the ring onto her finger. He looked at it for a second. "I never thought I'd be able to make this kind of promise to anyone. I think I could only ever make it to you." He lifted his eyes up to the ceiling. "And them."

She took his face in her hands. "I love you." Because love was a promise. Love was hope.

And no matter what a person lost, love could give and give and give.

Forever.

The End

If you enjoyed this book, please leave a review at your favorite online retailer! Even if it's just a sentence or two it makes all the difference.

Thanks for reading Christmas for the Deputy by Nicole Helm!

Discover your next romance at TulePublishing.com.

If you enjoyed *Christmas for the Deputy,*
you'll love the other book in....

The Bad Boys of Last Stand series

Book 1: *Homecoming for the Cowboy*

Book 2: *Christmas for the Deputy*
View the series here!

More books by Nicole Helm

Bride by Mistake

Keep Me, Cowboy

Ignite

Bride for Keeps

If you enjoyed *Christmas for the Deputy*, you'll love these other Last Stand Christmas books!

Christmas Flowers
by Sasha Summers

A Lone Star Christmas
by Justine Davis

Under the Mistletoe
by Eve Gaddy

About the Author

Nicole Helm writes down-to-earth contemporary romance—from farmers to cowboys, midwest to *the* west, she writes stories about people finding themselves and finding love in the process. She lives in Missouri with her husband and two sons, surrounded by light sabers, video games, and a shared dream of someday owning a farm.

Thank you for reading

Christmas for the Deputy

If you enjoyed this book, you can find more from all our great authors at TulePublishing.com, or from your favorite online retailer.

Made in the USA
Middletown, DE
13 May 2025

75494452R00125